THE DAYLIGHT
INTRUDER

DATE DUE

9-26-95			
GAYLORD			PRINTED IN U.S.A.

OTHER BOOKS
IN THE SERIES

MARGO MYSTERIES

THE
DAYLIGHT
INTRUDER

J. B. JENKINS

Thomas Nelson Publishers
Nashville

Published in Nashville, Tennessee, by Thomas
Nelson, Inc., and distributed in Canada by
Lawson Falle, Ltd., Cambridge, Ontario.

**Library of Congress
Cataloging-in-Publication Data**

Jenkins, Jerry B.
   [Karlyn]
   The daylight intruder / J.B. Jenkins.
     p. cm.—(Margo mysteries ; vol. 2)
   Previously published as: Karlyn. c1980.
   ISBN 0-8407-3210-4
   I. Title. II. Series: Jenkins, Jerry B.
  Margo mysteries ; vol. 2
  PS3560.E485D39 1991
  813'.54—dc20
                        90–45016
                           CIP

Printed in the United States of America
1 2 3 4 5 6 7 — 96 95 94 93 92 91

THE
DAYLIGHT
INTRUDER

ONE

Virginia Franklin would be sentenced today. As painful as that would be for her, not to mention her daughter, Margo, a major chapter in my life would echo shut with her cell door—and I couldn't deny that I was glad.

Margo was quiet, almost icy, as we drove to the Lake County, Illinois, Circuit Court with James Hanlon and Earl Haymeyer not far behind. The arraignment and brief trial had been as rough on Margo as everything that had led to her mother's confession. But the sentencing, which promised no surprises unless the judge had been stricken with some overwhelming compassion or—to read the newspaper accounts—some incredible stupidity the night before, would prove even rougher.

Amos Chakaris, the former Illinois secretary of state and semiretired lawyer representing Mrs. Franklin, had won several concessions in the case, in spite of heavy civic and media pressure to see the full brunt of the law fall on Judge Franklin.

Chakaris had so far kept her out of jail. The usual bond in such a case is about a quarter of a million dollars, of which the defendant must come up with ten percent. Probably because the defendant in this case was a Cook County circuit court judge, the Lake County judge quadrupled the figure

Mrs. Franklin's former husband, George, on whom she had tried to blame the murder at one point, offered to post the $100,000. She refused his offer, so he set up a legal defense fund for her. When he received virtually no contributions, he announced that an anonymous donor had come up with the money.

Her temporary freedom allowed Virginia no false optimism. During the more than four months since her original confession, she seemed to worry most about the conditions she would face at the women's facility in the Pontiac State Penitentiary.

She had not been a circuit judge in the criminal courts for sixteen years without knowing that she would be sentenced, pure and simple. A plea bargain to lessen the charge from first to second degree murder was successful, provided that Chakaris not seek any more concessions. He agreed, and the next day inadvertently broke his promise.

"Your Honor," he had said at the obligatory evidence trial, "there is the matter of protective custody when my client is incarcerated."

"Mr. Chakaris, I made it very clear yesterday that there would be precious few luxuries allowed in this hearing. On the other hand the court is grateful for the cooperation the defense has exhibited to this point in not dragging this out more than necessary."

"If Your Honor please," Chakaris continued, "I believe this is a matter of utmost urgency and see it as much more than a luxury. The very life of my client may depend on it."

"On protective custody?"

"Absolutely. Judge Franklin will encounter women in that facility whom she has sent there. And even the ones she hasn't sent there will know who she is and will be more than happy to strike back at authority by humiliating her and possibly even attacking her. I would request that Your

Honor consider stipulating that she be segregated from the general prison population."

The judge agreed to consider it, but there was little more to hope for other than the reduction of the charge. That probably would make the difference between a life sentence and one of ten to twenty years (with parole consideration allowed after three years, but highly unlikely).

The newspapers and the public had reacted as you would expect to a pious judge who not only murders her lover—who happened to be an assistant state's attorney—but then also tries another man for that very crime, scares her daughter by nearly having her killed, works with the syndicate to implicate her own husband, and avoids suspicion for nearly nine years.

Now her quick confession and eagerness to take her punishment rang hollow in everyone's ears. They wanted to see her all but strung up, and no Lake County judge was about to risk his reputation by slapping her wrist.

The judge had at first resisted Chakaris's plea for a reduced charge in exchange for her cooperation, but the prosecution encouraged him to concede it if she would implicate syndicate leaders as well. What it boiled down to was that all her collusion and related crimes were ignored, the charge was reduced, and the judge would consider having her segregated at Pontiac. That was as far as he would go. The sentencing itself would tell how tough and/or dramatic he wanted to be with a courtroom full of reporters.

Margo stared out the window on her side of the car. I reached across the back of the seat to touch her shoulder. I felt her relax until I said, "Well, what do you think will happen today?"

She turned sharply toward me and stared until I was forced to take my eyes from the road and return her gaze. When I looked back to watch the road, she said, "You make it sound like a basketball game. Who's gonna win?'"

"I didn't mean to make it sound that way, Margo. I just know you're as curious as I am about the possibilities."

"Curious? That's what you think I've been? Curious?"

"Margo, please," I said. "Don't accuse me of being insensitive. You know that even if it didn't come out right, I didn't mean anything by it."

She looked away again, and I felt as if a heat lamp had been turned off. "So what do you think will happen?" she asked. "Be honest. I want to know what you really think."

"I'm not optimistic," I admitted.

"I'm not either," she said. "What do Earl and Jim think?"

"The same."

"Wonderful," she said sadly.

The parking lot was crowded and the press was coming. By now they knew "Margo's guy" had been heavily involved in the investigation. The first parking place I found was too close to the surge of reporters. I backed out quickly and wheeled around to the back of the building.

It was no use; we weren't going to get inside without having to answer questions. "I really don't need this today," Margo said, as if she might need it some other time.

I would have thought we had been asked everything in the book and that the media would grow tired of us, but we got the same questions every time. "Is it true you're secretly married?"

"No."

"Are you living together?"

"No!"

"Are you going to be married?"

"I haven't been asked yet," Margo said.

"Are you going to ask her?"

"No comment."

"If he asks you, will you accept?"

"No comment."

"You mean you might not?"

"I mean I don't know. I'll think about it if it happens. Excuse us, please."

"Where will you live? What will you do? Do you think your mother will be sentenced for life?"

"Please!" I said. "Leave her alone. Let us through." But there was nowhere to walk.

"Do you think she'll get a life sentence?"

Now I was angry. "She can't get a life sentence on a second degree charge," I said. "You know that."

"Have you studied law? Are you really just an artist?"

I ignored the question, kept a firm grip on Margo's arm, and began walking through the crowd. Microphones were poked into our faces, and I heard one tap Margo's teeth. She recoiled and I drove a straight-arm into the reporter just as a muscular arm grabbed my own and led both of us through the crowd and into the building.

It was Earl Haymeyer and his boss, Jim Hanlon. The United States attorney towered over the wiry Haymeyer, and as soon as we were inside, the attention of the press turned to him. "Mr. Hanlon, is it true you'll be running for governor?"

"If I say yes, will you leave these kids alone?"

"Sure! Is it true?" By now we were safely inside the courtroom and Earl had returned to Hanlon's side. That night on the news, Chicagoans heard Hanlon's reply:

"No, I just wanted you to leave them alone. We already have a governor, and I have a big enough job for now." (It wasn't true. He had told us the night before at the hotel that he was going to enter the race.)

Margo had a rolled up *Daily Herald* in her purse, along with a dog-eared paperback copy of *Psalms and Proverbs*. She handed me the paperback and unrolled her paper, but somehow I wasn't in the mood for Scripture right then—any more than she was.

It wasn't that we didn't know where our strength came from. In the last several weeks we had read and studied and discussed more of the Bible than I, for one, had ever done in my life.

And Margo. She was the brand new Christian, yet she wanted so badly to offer some spiritual help to her mother and father that she ran circles around me in searching for answers. She read everything either of us could get our hands on, listened to tapes, and went to church every Sunday and sometimes during the week.

It had become more and more difficult to sneak away with Haymeyer or one of his men and get somewhere without being noticed, but that was part of the fun. It had even taken our minds off the ordeal we had been through and the fact that we would soon witness Margo's mother's sentencing.

And now here we were. At the crisis hour we wanted to read the paper. Maybe we had already found our answers and our strength. We didn't need to cram at the last minute. I set the book between us on the bench and read the paper over her shoulder.

FRANKLIN SENTENCE EXPECTED TODAY, the headline read. The article recapped the whole bizarre story and wondered at the turn of events that prompted a daughter who had "turned" on her mother to sit directly behind her in court and provide moral support.

Margo looked up from the paper when her mother came into court with Amos Chakaris, stood, and embraced her. No one would ever understand it; certainly not the press. Reporters were puzzled over my role in the whole affair until Margo one day had just blurted it out: "Philip is the one who encouraged me to do the right thing."

Once they had pounced on the fact that I had been involved from the beginning, they dragged out details of my having been allowed to hang around the investigation. Haymeyer even allowed once that I had been of some help and had showed "an instinct for our kind of work." I had been a minor celebrity for a few days, which was not at all like I had ever dreamed fame would be.

I was hounded more than ever, switched hotel rooms and phone numbers every few days, and could hardly go anywhere without a plan.

Margo and I had read the rehash of the story so many times that we instinctively knew how far into the articles to look for any new material. While Mrs. Franklin was deep into a quiet discussion with Chakaris, Margo and I locked our eyes onto the newspaper account of various experts' speculations about the length of the sentence.

Hanlon and Haymeyer slid into place beside Margo. "How you holding up, girl?" Earl asked. Margo had never liked his calling her that, but he seemed so fond of her that she decided not to say anything about it.

"I'm OK," she said, forcing a smile.

"And you, Picasso?" he said, leaning past her. I just nodded.

The judge entered and we stood.

TWO

"Hear ye, hear ye," the bailiff sang out, "the circuit court of Lake County, Illinois, is now in session, the honorable Judge Stephen Gregory presiding. You may be seated. The State of Illinois versus Virginia Franklin."

The prosecutors remained standing, as did Mrs. Franklin and Amos Chakaris. He was obviously worried, though this should have been a cut-and-dried case of admitted murder and a normal plea bargain to second degree. His hope was that by throwing his client upon the mercy of the court, he could get her the minimum sentence for that charge.

He had seen a lot of days in the courtroom, even more than his fifty-nine-year-old client. Chakaris, a swarthy, heavy man, was red-faced and sweating, in stark contrast to the defendant who was stylishly dressed as usual, hair done right, makeup just so, formally stern, standing rigidly.

At a meeting of all of us, except Mrs. Franklin, at the hotel the night before, Chakaris had told Haymeyer and Hanlon that he just didn't understand why Gregory wants to be so stubborn on the sentencing.

"Jim, Earl, you know it's customary in cases like this, where there's an early confession and plea and the usual amount of bargaining and concessions, for the judge to discuss the sentencing with both sides before the formal hearing. Why wouldn't he do that? Is he grandstanding? If he is, I'll appeal this crazy thing to the state supreme court and let the boys in Springfield decide if the guy is fit to sit on the bench."

"You'd appeal a case where your client has pleaded guilty?" Hanlon asked.

"I'd appeal the sentence, Jimmy. If the judge is so all-fired concerned about surprising everyone—us officers of the court included—with his sentence pronouncement, maybe the guy has a problem."

"Amos," Haymeyer broke in, "you know Gregory has an impeccable record. They wouldn't assign someone to a case like this who had a spot or blemish. The man is sound and fair."

"I know that, Earl," Chakaris said. "That's why I'm worried about the sentence. Virginia and I agreed a long time ago that by going this route we'd stand the best chance of getting the thing over as quickly as possible and get the best deal we can. If he's gonna pull some stiffer-than-appropriate sentence out of his hat tomorrow, I may be forced to drag the case even further."

"I hope not," Margo interrupted.

"Well, I hope not too, honey," Chakaris said. "But you wouldn't want your mother to take a worse sentence than she should just because of all the publicity this case has received, would you?"

"I have no idea what an appropriate sentence is for the crime and everything that went along with it," Margo said, defeated.

"She's right, Amos," Hanlon said. "You've gotta admit that a judge who hid her guilt for nine years—"

"I know already, Jim. I know. OK?" Chakaris said, a meaty hand in front of him. "I just don't like going into the courtroom unprepared and dreading a surprise. This poker face has served me well over the years, but I'm going to be uncomfortable tomorrow."

And he was. "Will the parties approach the bench?" Judge Gregory intoned now. Chakaris stepped aside to let Virginia Franklin move toward the bench first. His eyes darted, his lips were pursed. A nice minimum sentence with parole consideration after three years would be a victory, he had often said.

The assistant prosecutor had spoken little during the proceedings, but the brief closing statement had fallen to him. His boss would ride the political wings of putting away Judge Franklin, and he would cut his own teeth on this scrap. "The people of Illinois are grateful to the defense for its cooperation in these proceedings. We feel it has contributed to the efficiency and economy of the hearings."

"Mr. Chakaris?"

"Thank you, Your Honor, and thank you, counselor. I do wish to speak, yes." The big man grasped Mrs. Franklin's elbow. "My client is guilty. She is remorseful. She is repentant—"

"If I may interrupt, Mr. Chakaris," the judge said. "You are aware, of course, that the verdict was handed down at the last hearing and that the sentence I am about to pronounce has already been decided upon. I would ask that your closing remarks not in any way resemble a further attempt to petition the bench on behalf of your client."

"Forgive me, Your Honor, but it is most unusual that neither side has been informed in advance of the sentence, and I fear that any objections I may have after the fact will be futile unless I take the case to Springfield."

"Mr. Chakaris, I find it regrettable that you are now marring what have been most expedient hearings with open threats to appeal a decision you have not even yet heard."

Chakaris sighed loudly and gestured with his free hand. "I admit that I sound desperate and pessimistic, but this is most unusual. We have no inkling whatever of the possible sentence. I feel at a loss to not be able to challenge it."

"May I remind counsel that you submitted that any and all other charges be dropped in lieu of the murder charge if Mrs. Franklin would turn state's evidence on those matters?"

"Which she did, sir."

"And mightn't anyone in her predicament, Mr. Chakaris? You also asked at the eleventh hour that I consider having her segregated from the general prison population."

"And I hope you have, Your Honor."

"Of course I have, and I am pleased to be able to say that it will be so stipulated, but that is precisely what has delayed my decision on the exact sentence until shortly before this hearing."

"If Your Honor would grant, could we recess to chambers so that we might react to the sentence before it is read in open court?"

"Mr. Chakaris, you are acting like a child before his birthday party. You can't stand the suspense."

"The analogy hardly fits," Chakaris replied. "I'm certainly not looking forward to this surprise, and I pray you aren't looking forward to springing it on us."

"That was entirely out of order, counselor."

"I'm sorry, Your Honor. I withdraw the statement and ask that it be stricken from the record."

"I'm going to have it stricken from the record," the judge

said, nodding to the court reporter, "but let me take you back to law school first. You have been a respected barrister and public official for more years than I have been on the bench, and you should know that it is I, not you, who asks that remarks be stricken from the record. And it is I, not you, who suggests recesses to my chambers. Is that understood?"

"Yes, sir," Chakaris said without emotion. "May my client speak?"

"Of course. Mrs. Franklin?"

Virginia Franklin had not spoken in the courtroom during any of the hearings. Even the guilty plea was entered by Chakaris. "I am throwing myself on the mercy of this court," she said. The judge nodded impatiently, looking helplessly to Chakaris. Suddenly the old fire came back to Mrs. Franklin. "Is there a problem with my statement already?" she challenged.

"No, ma'am," the judge said. "Except that this entire hearing is becoming redundant. We know the crime, we know the plea, we know the evidence, we know the verdict. We even know, and have been reminded of it every time your counsel has spoken, that you are repentant and remorseful and are throwing yourself on the mercy of this court. Do you have anything new to add to the record? Because if not, I would like to pronounce sentence, and I wish not to have you or your attorney respond. Is there anything else?"

Chakaris and Mrs. Franklin looked at each other. Chakaris raised his eyebrows and shrugged. To him any further discussion was pointless. "If Your Honor would indulge me," Mrs. Franklin said, "and not make it any more difficult by looking condescendingly upon me, I would like to enter one more statement into the record."

The judge looked down at his papers and made some notes. Without looking up, he said, "You may proceed with a *brief* statement."

"I just want to express my gratitude and love to my daughter—for her courage and for doing what she knew was right in spite of everything." Mrs. Franklin's voice quavered and Margo's eyes filled. "She helped me put an end to a nine-year nightmare, and I find myself strangely thankful."

The judge looked up, suddenly formal and silent. "Thank you very much," he said finally, his eyes scanning the principals before him. "Is there anything else at all?" No one responded. The courtroom was silent except for the swishing of the artists' sketch pads and the scribbling of reporters' pens.

"Mrs. Virginia Franklin, you have confessed to and been found guilty by the people of the state of Illinois of second degree murder in the November 11, 1970, murder of Richard Wanmacher. I have taken into consideration your cooperation and plea in this matter and wish to remind you again of the extraordinary generosity of the prosecution in reducing the charge.

"However, due to the nature of your station in life, which for many years had been as a circuit judge in the criminal courts of Cook County, Illinois, I find the crime and your subsequent actions equally reprehensible. You need no lecture on why the leaders of society ought also to be its moral models.

"To try a man for a murder that you yourself committed, to then attempt to implicate others of even your own immediate family, and to force investigators to the hilt before finally coming forward to acknowledge that you were without further recourse, constitutes an arrogant thumbing of your nose at the laws of this state, the laws you were sworn to uphold.

"It is, therefore, my ruling that you shall be immediately turned over to the custody of the Illinois Department of Corrections to be imprisoned in the women's facility at the Illinois State Penitentiary at Pontiac for a period of not less than twenty-five years."

THREE

Amos Chakaris caught a stumbling Virginia Franklin in one tree trunk of an arm, but his objection and the judge's refusal to act upon it could not be heard over the commotion. Reporters sprinted for the phones, observers for their cars. Judge Gregory, who would be the darling of the six o'clock news, left in a flourish.

Margo tried to get to her mother but was pushed away by Chakaris himself who didn't realize who it was and was merely trying to protect Mrs. Franklin. "We'll appeal the sentence, we'll appeal it," he kept whispering to her.

"Mother, I'll see you tomorrow," Margo shouted as a corrections officer guided Mrs. Franklin away from Chakaris and the crowd.

Haymeyer and Hanlon's unmarked sedan awaited us as we stepped out a side door. "Get in," Earl said. "Jim says we should take you back to the hotel and bring you back here later for your car." A quick glance at the horde of media people surrounding my car convinced me of the wisdom of that idea. We climbed into the backseat, and Haymeyer pulled around to another exit where the enraged Chakaris stormed out and jumped in without a second thought.

We were several blocks from the courthouse before he asked, "What am I doing with you guys?"

"You really want to go back there and get your car now, Amos?" Hanlon asked. The big man shifted to look out the back window, nearly knocking me into Margo's lap. "Sure don't," he said. "Sure enough don't."

"Well, it'll all be over by tomorrow morning," Haymeyer said. "Philip, I want you and Margo to feel free to stay the night in your rooms." It was just details, but when he was through with business, there was nothing to talk about except the hearing. And no one wanted to do that.

Margo finally broke the ice. "Are you going to appeal, Amos?"

"Well, frankly, there's no hurry," he said. "Even if it were reduced to the minimum she wouldn't be eligible for even parole consideration until three years. That gives us that long to make noise."

"Three years," Margo repeated. "When can I visit her?"

"You can see her briefly before she goes tomorrow," Chakaris said. "And then you won't be able to see her again for three weeks. Then you can see her a half hour a week after that." Margo stared at him. "I'm as upset about this as you are, Margo," he said.

"I doubt it."

"I suppose you're right," he admitted. "She isn't my mother. But I hope you know I did everything I could. I believe we have a real shot at getting the sentence reduced. There didn't seem to be many grounds for his invoking the maximum."

Margo raised both arms and let them drop. "I know you did everything you could, Amos, and I'm grateful. It's all in your hands now. I'll be moving to Pontiac to be as close to her as possible. She'll need me. This will be too much for her. I don't know how she'll be able to stand it. I'd like to go to my room for a while."

Hanlon, Haymeyer, Chakaris, and I glanced nervously at each other. "Let her go," Hanlon whispered to me. Haymeyer spoke to her.

"You going to call your father?"

"I suppose. I know now why he didn't want to be in court for any of this." She dug in her pockets for her room key, coming up with it in her left hand and a folded piece of paper in her right. "What's this?" she asked, looking at us as if we had planted it there.

She opened it and read silently. "Earl, look at this."

"Where'd you get it?" he asked.

"I don't know. It wasn't there when I left this morning."

"What is it?" I asked, miffed that I had not been the first one she showed it to. Hanlon followed me to Haymeyer's side and we read it together silently:

"Margo:

"I desperately need you and your boyfriend's help. I beg you not to turn me down. If you will listen, call me tonight at 9 at the phone number below. Karlyn M."

"What do you make of it, Earl?" Hanlon asked.

"Someone must have given it to her in the crowd today," Earl said. "Either when the press was surrounding you two or right at the end of the hearing. You don't know who it was or what you might be setting yourself up for if you reply to it, so I wouldn't advise doing anything with it until you know who this Karlyn M. is."

"How am I supposed to determine that?"

"I don't know," Haymeyer admitted. "But let me check out a few things while Jim takes Amos and Philip back to their cars. You go ahead to your room and call your father and get some rest. We'll talk later, OK?"

We hardly spoke on the way back to the courtroom parking lot. Amos was one whipped lawyer. He just sat shaking his head. We'd been through it so many times that we were sick of it. My original intuition had been right. Mrs. Franklin would be transported to Pontiac the next day, and I would be done with it for a while.

The only thing that bothered me was that Margo had said she was going to move to Pontiac. Surely I could talk her out of that. There was little reason to move that far away when you could see a prisoner only a half hour a week anyway.

"What do you make of the note?" I asked Hanlon.

"Got me," he said. "Could be a prank. I don't even want to think about it. It isn't that I don't care for you and Margo as much as ever, Philip, but this one is not likely to fall under the jurisdiction of my office, and frankly I'm glad not to have to worry about it."

It made me feel good to know I wasn't alone in my relief over the end of the Virginia Franklin case. "But why is Earl getting involved then?" I asked.

"Oh, I wouldn't say he's getting involved. He'll probably just call Larry Shipman, his journalist friend, and see if he knows anyone who was shooting videotape when you two walked into court today. Maybe he'll see someone on the tape who could have slipped Margo the note. If it happened in the courtroom at the end, though, there'll be no record of it."

"How can Earl stay out of it?" I asked. "He's a born detective, isn't he?"

"I hope not," Hanlon said.

"Why?"

"Because I want to talk him into hanging up the gumshoes and being in charge of security for my campaign. If I win, Earl can have any law enforcement job he wants in Springfield. I'll probably endorse ol' Amos here for secretary of state again."

Chakaris, who had been dozing, opened one eye and grunted. "I'm through with politics," he said. "Seventy-one is too old for the courtroom too. I was like a senile old fool today."

"Nonsense," Hanlon scolded. "You did what any self-respecting lawyer would have done, and you'll look good on the record too. It'll probably help you get the sentence reduced."

"Do you really think so, Jimmy?" Chakaris asked, gratefully. "You always were a good law student."

I had the idea when I shook hands with Chakaris in the parking lot that I might never see him again. He would quit practicing law except to appeal Mrs. Franklin's sentence. As for me, I didn't know what I would do.

I followed Hanlon back to the hotel I'd stayed in for the four-and-a-half months of arraignments and hearings. Hanlon and Haymeyer had moved us all out of hiding downtown once the Mafia leaders began to be picked up on Mrs. Franklin's information. That way, too, we were close to the court. When Mrs. Franklin was safely on her way to Pontiac the next day, our security would be pulled off and we'd be on our own.

That would be fine with me. I was tired of being trailed or accompanied everywhere. Hanlon checked out of the suite where the bunch of us had met—along with our security agents—almost every night for the last several weeks. Now only Margo and I and our 'round-the-clock guards were left in the hotel from the original group.

Haymeyer was still on the phone when I entered my room. "Philip's here now," he said. "We'll be leaving shortly. Thanks, Larry. We'll see ya."

I dropped onto the bed. "Earl, please tell me we're not going anywhere," I said.

"You don't have to if you don't want to," he said. "But

Shipman has a friend who shot a lot of tape while you and Margo were going into court today. He'll put it on a machine anytime we want to see it."

"What time is it?" I asked.

"Just after three."

"Can I take a nap first?"

"And what am I gonna do, lover boy? Sit here and watch? I don't have a room in this joint anymore, you know. And this case is unofficial anyway. This is on my own time. I'm just as curious about this note as you are."

"Maybe more so. I wish it would go away. I'm intrigued, sure, but who needs more excitement than I've had in the last several months? I just want to relax a while, get back to my drawing, decide what I'm going to do about Margo."

"Well, it's up to you, Philip," Earl said. "Though somehow I can't see you letting this one rest until you find out what it's all about."

"Me? Why?"

"Because that's just the way you are. You're like me. The real motive behind my work is curiosity. Sure, it's helpful to society. I try to keep the streets safe and all that. But the fun of the job is in finding the answers. The search. I'll tell you what—if that isn't what you like, how about if I go see the tape and let you know if I find anything, hm?"

Haymeyer stood and pulled on his coat.

"Not on your life," I said. I called Margo to tell her we'd be back by early evening.

"Daddy took the news well," she said. "I think he's going to be all right. I'll try to start seeing more of him now."

"You going to go to bed early and sleep through?" I asked.

"I don't think so. I'll probably be ready for a little company by the time you two get back."

"Tell her to stay up and we'll take her out for a nice dinner," Haymeyer said. She liked the idea.

As Earl and I got into the car, it hit me that Margo sounded as confused about the future as I was. How was she going to see more of her father in Winnetka and her mother in Pontiac? And where did she think I'd be all that time, or did she care? We'd been thrown together so dramatically and unrealistically that we had never had time to sort out our relationship.

We had grown dependent upon each other, and there was no doubt in anyone's mind that we cared about each other. Although we had never talked about it, everyone who knew us considered it a foregone conclusion that we would wind up married when this was all over.

I wasn't sure how either of us felt about that. Maybe we both realized that we needed time to recuperate and perhaps even to be apart for a while. I hoped that everything I felt for Margo had not been artificial because of the situation. I didn't know what she was feeling for me anymore.

I had learned enough about Chicago to know that when Haymeyer exited east off the Edens Expressway onto Tower Road and took it to Glencoe Road, we were taking the long way to Larry Shipman and the television station. "Where are we going, Earl?" I asked.

"Larry isn't expecting us for another few minutes. There's something I want to show you, anyway."

FOUR

Haymeyer pulled onto a side street and parked in front of a quaint two-story building about a half block long that housed a drugstore on one end and women's boutique on the other. Various shops occupied the middle properties on the first floor while the second story housed an optometrist, two dentists, a podiatrist, and some attorney's offices.

"There are also six flats upstairs," Haymeyer said. "Pretty nice too. Only one occupied right now. The others were just redecorated and should be filled soon."

"How do you know all this?"

"I own the building."

"*You* own this building? I thought you lived downtown and worked sixteen hours a day."

"I do. Or at least I did. I've made pretty good money the last few years, and I've hardly had any expenses except eating and sleeping. I don't even own a car, or at least I didn't until a few days ago when I ordered one. I've always driven 'company' cars."

"You know, Earl, it embarrasses me how little I know about you. After all the time we've spent together, I realize we have been so wrapped up in Margo and her mother that we never really talked about you. Are you married?"

"Widower."

"I'm sorry."

"It's all right. I was an idealist who worshiped her and haven't been able to even think of anyone replacing her. I have friends, but no one special."

"How long has it been?"

"Six years. And we were married six years too."

"No children?"

"One. Institutionalized. I see him now and then. He doesn't know me. Junior."

"Sounds like a lonely life."

"I don't let it get lonely, Philip. I work all the time and I love my work. Always have."

"Then what's all this?" I asked, waving at the building.

"Just a little security and a place to live. I had money stashed away that inflation was eating up, so now I've got something that will provide rent income and will allow me to fail in my own business."

"Your own business? C'mon, are you going to make me drag this out of you sentence by sentence?"

Haymeyer laughed. "I guess not. Look at this," he said, pulling a letter from his pocket. The envelope was addressed to Mr. James A. Hanlon, U.S. Attorney for Northern Illinois, State of Illinois Bldg., Chicago, IL. "You can read it," he said.

"Dear Jim:

"It's been rewarding and unforgettable. I'm flattered by your hints that I would always have a place with you wherever you go and whatever you do, but you know as well as I do that I'm a detective first and foremost and always.

"I wish you the best in your run for the governorship, will help you in any way I can, and would bet against all odds that you'll win and be a great one. Maybe when you become president I'll consider the leadership of the FBI!

"Meanwhile, wish me luck on what I've always wanted to do. I've got an income-producing property in a great location and I'm going into private practice. 'EH Detective Agency/Private Investigations' has a ring to it, don't you think?

"You'll know who to come to when you need it done right. And I promise not to take any penny ante cases like trailing unfaithful spouses.

"Thanks for understanding, Jim. I'd like this effective April 1.

"As always, Earl Haymeyer."

"That's less than a month away," I said. "How's he going to react?"

"You can never tell with Jim Hanlon," Earl said. "He may pout a little, but he won't try to talk me out of it. We've always been real close on the job and not so close off the job. He's not a meddler. He'll want me to stay, which will make me feel good, but he won't make me feel guilty for leaving."

"You can't ask for more than that."

"You sure can't," Earl said, pulling away. "I'll show you the building sometime soon. You're going to need an apartment anyway, aren't you?"

"I don't know, Earl. I appreciate the offer, but I don't even have a source of income right now. If I'm going to stay near Margo, I'll have to get back to Atlanta and move my stuff. I don't know where she's going to be, and I don't think she does either. If she's bound and determined to move to Pontiac, I may settle up here after all. I can't see living there. I would have very little work outside a metropolitan area."

"We're going to have to talk about your career," Earl said. "Maybe tonight after dinner."

It was chilly by the time we rolled into the Channel 8 parking lot in the Loop. Larry Shipman let us in by a side entrance. I had met him early in the Virginia Franklin investigation when Hanlon had used him as a plant in the jail to bring back information. Shipman was a sort of freelance everything. He hung around newspapers and TV stations until they gave him work to do, and he also worked with Earl and Jim when they needed him.

"I looked at the tapes," Shipman said. "Tell me what you're looking for and I can probably punch right to it."

"Well," Haymeyer began, "Margo found something in her pocket when she got back from the hearing."

"Got it," Shipman said, beaming.

"You're unbelievable," Haymeyer said, shaking his head. "Are you serious?"

"Of course! You know I don't kid around."

They both laughed. "You know," Larry continued as he fast forwarded the videotape machine, "I could work for you and Jim for nothing, just for those appreciative exclamations you come out with now and then."

"I'll remember that," Earl said.

"Please don't," Shipman said, stopping the machine and restarting it at regular speed. It was weird to watch myself opening the door for Margo and then trying to move into the building before the press closed in.

"You see, Earl," Shipman said, "there are several people in this crowd who are not press. Many with no recorders or cameras or microphones or even notepads. They are just bystanders who see the commotion and want to be in on it. Now watch. As they realize that they can't hear anything anyway, they begin to fall away. Then all you've got is the core of the reporters and maybe just one or two outsiders."

Larry cut the sound and punched the slow motion button. "Now watch carefully," he said. Incredulous, I saw the press crowd in close enough to jam the microphones in our faces and saw myself build to a boil in slow motion. Larry cut the speed one more time until it was coming an image at a time.

A microphone tapped Margo's tooth, she jerked back, and my arm shot out toward the reporter. Just as I made contact Margo and I were scooped up by Haymeyer and Hanlon and steered through the crowd. "Did you see it?" Shipman asked.

"Yeah," I said. "I nearly flattened that reporter."

"You missed it," Shipman said, giggling. "Did you see it, Earl?"

"Yes, but I wouldn't be too hard on Philip. He's still a kid in this business, but he has potential. Run it back again, Lar. And, Philip, this time don't watch your own performance. Look for what we're looking for. The note wasn't placed in Margo's mouth or in your hand, was it?"

"No," I said sheepishly.

Shipman backed up the tape a few seconds and ran it again. The microphone hit Margo's mouth and I made my move, but this time I forced my eyes from the action and watched Margo's coat. "Right there," we said in unison. A short blonde woman, about twenty-five, slipped the note into Margo's pocket just as Margo's head snapped back. The woman was nearly bowled over by Hanlon as he and Haymeyer pushed through behind us.

Shipman stopped the tape just as the woman crossed in front of the camera. In spite of the emotional strain obvious on her face, she was striking. She wore a light trench coat of dark blue and a thin scarf at her throat. She was made up like a model, and her yellow hair was cropped close and hung just short of her shoulders.

"Not bad, huh?" Shipman asked, but I didn't know if he meant the girl or his work.

"Not bad, Larry," Earl said. "Now can we jump ahead

and see if the cameraman got a shot of everyone leaving the courtroom?"

"He did."

"Then let's see if she was in the group."

"She wasn't."

"Boy," Haymeyer said, "you don't miss a trick, do you?"

"Nope, and thanks for the compliment."

"That was no compliment. That was next week's pay. Anyway, if she wasn't in the courtroom, she probably had no interest in the trial."

"Does she look like a Karlyn?" I asked.

"I dunno," Shipman said. "What does a Karlyn look like?"

I shrugged. "I just wonder if she is the writer of the note or just the messenger."

"Good question, Philip," Haymeyer said. "If you went to work with me, would you settle for compliments instead of paychecks?"

Shipman laughed. "Anything else I can do for you gents?" he asked.

"Nope, we gotta go," Haymeyer said. "You'll hear from me soon."

"Why? Is this on Hanlon's budget?"

"Even if it's not, this one deserves more than compliments, wouldn't you say?"

"I won't argue with that. What was in the note, by the way?"

"Can't tell you yet. Trust me."

"Always," Shipman said.

We called Margo before we left Chicago, allowing her enough time to be ready when we arrived. "Tell her to dress up," Earl said. "I'll take you guys to a place we haven't had time for until now."

She looked only a little less tense than she had at the trial, but she said she felt a lot better. "I just don't know what I'm going to do now," she said.

"Neither do I," I said. "Why don't we postpone thinking about it until after dinner. Let's try to put our brains in neutral until we're ready to make some plans."

"I was hoping you'd take charge," she said, leaning her head on my shoulder. "Even if taking charge means postponing action, that's fine with me. There are just a few things I have to do. I have to get out of my hotel room, get back to Atlanta, pack my stuff, move it to Pontiac, and find a job and a place to live."

"I hate to put a wet blanket on all those wonderful plans," Haymeyer said, "but you seem to be ignoring a little responsibility that rolls around at nine tonight, just a couple of hours from now."

"Do you really think I should call this girl, Earl? I'm not ready for any more escapades for a few years."

"Read me the second sentence in that note again," Earl said.

Margo dug for the note, then read aloud: "I beg you not to turn me down."

"Can you ignore that?" Haymeyer asked.

Margo looked at me and sighed with resignation. "I was desperate once too. I'm glad you didn't ignore me."

FIVE

Earl took us to an exclusive French restaurant in one of the luxurious hotels near O'Hare International Airport. It didn't take long for us to break our promise not to talk about the future until after dinner.

"Your plans don't seem to include me," I said.

"Sure they do. You dragged me up here from Atlanta in your own car, and I assume I have a round-trip ticket." She poked me in the ribs to assure me she was kidding. "Seriously, Philip, there are so many things to think about now that I don't know what to do about us. Don't you agree that we need time to just think it through?"

"No doubt," I said. "It'll probably cost me, though."

"Cost you what?"

"Cost me you."

"Why do you say that?"

"Oh, you'll start thinking about the whole situation and realize that our relationship was forced from the start. Out of sight, out of mind, end of Philip."

"Oh, poor baby," she said.

"Shed me a tear," Earl said.

"Keep out of this," I said. "How can a guy have a pity party with you two around?"

"Want us to leave?"

"Cute."

It was eight o'clock and we were eating. We had avoided much talk of Karlyn, other than a description of her for Margo. "What should I say to her?"

"I think you ought to try to shock her," Haymeyer said. "Unless she tells you what she wants right away and gives you her full name, treat her as a nuisance and tell her what you liked about what she wore today."

"Really?"

"Sure, it'll scramble her mind a little. Force her out into the open. Why didn't she come to you openly?"

By eight forty-five we were racing down the Kennedy Expressway toward the Loop. "What if I don't call her in time?" Margo asked.

"All the better," Earl said. "Let her wonder a little. We don't want to be too late, but I do want to do it from Jim's office where we can tape and also listen in."

"Jim won't mind?" I asked. "Since it's not federal business?"

"I'll pay for it," Haymeyer said.

"And who'll pay you?" Margo asked. "Moneybags here and I are in no condition to be engaging a private detective."

"Consider it a free introductory offer," Earl said. He winked at me and Margo cocked her head.

"You'll have to let Earl tell you," I said.

"Later," he said.

Margo shook her head. "I can't keep up with you two."

Hanlon was there when we arrived, surprising Earl. Haymeyer filled him in and asked if he could use the phone equipment. "You know you don't have to ask," Jim said. "Especially considering what I'm going to ask you tomorrow."

"You're going to ask me tomorrow?" Earl said.

"Yup."

"Then I'd better give you this tonight."

"Should I read it now?"

"Not if it's going to change your decision about the phones."

"It won't, but I have the feeling this is one I should save until I get home."

"Suit yourself."

"I'm leaving now, Earl. Let me know how this thing turns out. And do lock up. I'm sorry. I know I don't have to tell you that, of all people."

"You're right, boss. You know me by now." The two shook hands, almost as if Hanlon had already read the letter. He might as well have. He knew what it contained.

"If I know Jim," Earl said a few minutes later, "he won't be able to wait until he gets home." He moved toward the window and looked down on Hanlon waiting for his car to be delivered from the underground garage. Margo and I peeked over his shoulder.

Hanlon opened the envelope and read the letter under a streetlight. He looked up from it and just stared across the street at nothing. He let both arms drop, the envelope in one hand and the letter in the other. His shoulders sagged wearily as he stood motionless in the cool spring air.

He crumpled the envelope and tossed it into a trash can, then carefully refolded the letter and slipped it into his breast pocket. "Get on the phone, Margo," Earl said. "We've got work to do."

Margo dialed the number and Earl started the machinery. He and I listened in on extensions in the same room. The number rang and rang, six times, then seven. "If she answers now, hang up immediately," Haymeyer said.

Margo shot him a puzzled look.

"Just do it," he said. "You don't want to be made a fool of. We don't know who this is or what she wants. We need to take the upper hand right away." The phone rang for the tenth time. And then she answered.

"This is Karlyn," she said in a whisper. "Who is this?"

Haymeyer motioned for Margo to hang up, which she did, reluctantly.

"That's good," Earl said. "No problem. We know she's there and we can call her back. We'll train her to answer immediately or she'll get no cooperation. This time I want you to talk to her only if she answers within the first three rings."

We waited a few minutes, then Margo dialed again. Karlyn answered on the fifth ring; Margo hung up before she could say anything.

"See how this puts us in the driver's seat?" Earl asked. "She had us over a barrel, and now we've got her wondering if she's going to hear from us at all."

"Us?" Margo said. "She doesn't even know about you."

"All the better. Call again."

Margo dialed. Karlyn answered immediately but said nothing.

Haymeyer put his finger to his lips. "Don't hang up," he mouthed. "But do make her talk first."

Margo waited.

"This is Karlyn. Who's this?"

"Who did you expect?" Margo said, surprisingly calm.

Haymeyer closed his eyes and gave her the "perfect" sign with his finger and thumb. He was amazed. She was doing well even without his coaching.

"Is this Margo?"

"This is Margo."

Margo was melting. It was against her nature to make someone squirm, and she was obviously about to make herself available to Karlyn. But before she could, Haymeyer repeated his silence signal.

"Are you the Margo whose mother is a . . . I mean your mother was sent to . . . was in court today?"

"Yes, my mother is the judge who murdered a man, and you know who I am because you saw me today. You were wearing a blue coat. Karlyn, what can I do for you?"

"I'm in trouble and I need help," she said quickly. "When you were in trouble, someone helped you. Will you help me?"

"I don't know. What kind of help do you need?"

"I can't tell you by phone. Will you meet me?"

"Where?"

Suddenly Karlyn was suspicious. "Is anyone listening in on this?" she asked.

Haymeyer shook his head, but Margo said, "Yes." Haymeyer winced.

"At least you're honest," Karlyn said. "Who's listening in?"

"Philip."

Haymeyer motioned for me not to say anything.

". . . and a friend named Earl," Margo said. Haymeyer rolled his eyes up in disbelief. Karlyn hung up.

Margo immediately began to redial, but Haymeyer cut her off. "Let's not press her," he said. "She needs us a lot more than we need her. She's made contact, and if we let her sweat it out, she'll be back."

"But she doesn't even know our number," Margo said. "Why do you insist on tormenting her?"

"I'm not trying to torment her, Margo. But this woman may wrap her tentacles around your life and bleed you to death emotionally before she'll tell you what it's all about. You must show her that you want to help but that you won't be taken advantage of. Actually, this is none of my business. You showed me the note, but you didn't ask my help. I'll understand if you want me to stay out of it."

Margo appealed to me with a look. "It's up to you," I said. "This is more hassle than you need right now. Earl can only help."

"Of course I want your help, Earl," Margo said. "I just want to feel free to question you, even to challenge you sometimes. Is that asking too much?"

"Not at all. Let's call Karlyn back and tell her that she can either tell you what her problem is now, over the phone, or she'll have to wait at least a week to meet you because you have personal matters to attend to."

"Which is true," I added.

"It certainly is," Margo said.

When Margo called again, Karlyn sounded fearful. "Do you want to help me or not?"

"I'm perfectly willing to help you," Margo said, "because someone helped me when I needed it. But I'm afraid I'm going to have to be just as firm with you as my helper was with me. I will not meet you alone because I don't know who you are or what your intentions are. And I need to know your full name."

"I'm Karlyn May."

"At least one person will be with me when I meet you, and it will have to be a place of my choosing. It will not be before a week from today, so if you need help more quickly than I can give it, you should look for it somewhere else."

Karlyn was silent for a long time. "I'll wait," she said finally. "Call me a week from today at eleven A.M. at this number, and I'll meet you and whoever else you trust anywhere you say." She suddenly sounded fragile. "And thank you very much."

Haymeyer was happy. "You did well, girl. Very, very well. I'm as mystified as you are, but at least we've got Karlyn May playing on our turf now, not hers."

"The trick now is to keep this off my mind for the next week," Margo said. "I'm going to have to count on you to help me with that, Philip."

I said I'd do what I could but that I thought the best thing to do now was for Earl to get us back to our hotel where we'd switch to the custody of our security agents for the last time.

"It's still early," Earl said. "At least let me show Margo my building first."

SIX

Margo readily agreed because she figured she would get the scoop on what Earl and I had been hinting at before. She was right. Only she got more than she bargained for. And so did I.

A fancy set of keys released the burglar alarm so Earl, the new landlord, could show us around. It was impressive. He told Margo he planned to live in the building while letting a real estate firm handle the business of collecting rents, hiring out repair work and complaint answering, and generally running the place.

"And this is where my office will be," he said, flipping on a bank of second floor lights to illuminate a huge room, bare except for a set of furniture that had not even been uncrated yet.

"What do you need an office for, if you're not going to run the building?" Margo asked.

"You'll see," Earl said. "This kind of thing excites me. I love new equipment and setting things up. Since I've never had my own office or business before, this is better yet. The sign painter comes tomorrow."

"The sign painter?" Margo said.

"To put my name on the door. In old-fashioned block lettering it'll say, 'EH Detective Agency/Private Investigations.'"

"Why old-fashioned?" Margo wondered. "You're a modern-type detective, aren't you?"

"Oh, sure, I use modern equipment and techniques, but I never let them get in the way of good, old-fashioned hard work and horse sense. This business is nothing like you see on television where the guy squeals around in a hot car shooting at everybody in sight. The majority of cases are solved by persistence and know-how."

Earl tore the cartons away from his furniture and revealed equipment that would fit the lettering on the door. It was new, obviously expensive stuff designed like the furniture of the thirties. He had a rolltop desk, Bank of England chairs, a ceiling fan, even quaint desk lamps.

"Well, Earl Haymeyer," I said, "if you aren't just an eccentric old cop after all."

"You didn't know that?" he said with a grin. "The suit and the briefcase threw you off, did they? Well, I'm more eccentric than this. Want to see where I sleep?"

"I'm not so sure."

Earl led us to a tiny apartment next to his office. The furnishings were sparse—though tastefully arranged—consisting of a single bed lodged next to an open window and covered with sheets, one electric blanket, and a pillow; a dresser and mirror; a table and wood chair; and a huge easy chair.

On one side of the room was a gigantic walk-in closet ("where I store everything I own and my meager wardrobe") and a full bath. The place was carpeted, painted, papered, and cozy.

"I love it," Margo said. "But why the open window?"

"Just another of my eccentricities," Earl explained. "I always sleep next to an open window and crank the blanket up as high as I need to."

"By 'always,' I assume you mean during reasonable weather?" Margo said.

"I mean always. In the summertime the window is wide open and I don't need the blanket. In the winter, when the windchill factor is way below zero, the window may be open only an eighth of an inch and I bury myself under the blanket with just my nose sticking out for air. Ah, you don't want to hear it. Suffice it to say, I like fresh air, keeping cool, and sleeping comfortably."

"What are your days like, living alone?" I asked.

"Pretty structured. I read the paper in my easy chair, first thing every morning. I skip breakfast and have my other two meals either out or delivered from a greasy spoon down the street. When the office is opened in a few days, I'll eat them there instead of here."

"It's neat, Earl," Margo said. "It really is. Right now I wouldn't mind a little structure in *my* life."

Margo and I waited in the car while Earl locked up and left a note for his new secretary in case she arrived at the office before he did in the morning.

"I need to tell you, Margo," I said, "that I can't see my moving to Pontiac, even though I don't look forward to being apart from you."

"I know, Philip," she said, taking my hand. "I want to be with you, too, but Mother needs me. I know it's not fair to you. You need to be near a big city so you'll have enough work. Maybe this will be good for us. You stay in Atlanta and I'll stay near Mother. If we're meant to be together, it will happen."

It wasn't that I disagreed with her—in fact, she made sense. "But Atlanta is an awfully long way from Pontiac," I said. "It would mean expensive phone bills and long trips to see you."

"Maybe you'll decide you don't want to see me."

"Or maybe you'll decide you don't want me to," I said. We stared at each other while we tried to put words into each other's mouths that we really didn't want to hear.

"That's not really what we want, is it?" I said. Margo looked down and shook her head.

Earl returned and started the car.

"I want to be near you and I want to be near Mother," Margo continued. "I really have no choice."

"But *you* do, Philip," Haymeyer interrupted.

"Sure. I can move to Pontiac if I want to, but how will I survive?"

"But you don't have to stay in Atlanta either," Earl said. "Chicago would be a ten times better market for you. Why do you think I brought you two whipped puppies tonight? To show you my soon-to-be office and my eccentricities?"

Margo and I looked at each other. "So what are you driving at, Earl?" she said.

"I need Philip," he said. "I've got clerical help coming from an agency, but I can't afford any more personnel. I don't know how the business will go and, frankly, I need a partner I don't have to pay much."

"Earl," I said, "I love the kind of work you do and I suppose if I had to choose and could start my life again, I wouldn't care if I didn't have artistic ability and could just study crime detection. But I do. I'm an artist, born and trained. I know nothing about your work."

"But you just said you love it, and that's oozed from you since we first met. You've been a stumbler and a bumbler just like all of us at first, but you caught on fast. You know people. You understand them. Best of all, you're curious. I know you couldn't just give up your art, any more than I could give up sleeping next to an open window in the winter. That's why I have a proposal."

"You've had this all planned out—what you were going

to say and everything?" Margo asked, admiration in her voice.

"I've thought about it a lot, yes."

"So, let's hear it," I said.

Earl accelerated onto the expressway. "I've held open one apartment, almost identical to mine. It's just down the hall from my office, maybe twenty steps. I could rent it tomorrow with no trouble, but I'll let you have it for as long as you work for me. I'll teach you the business, and I can give you a thousand dollars a month."

"I can't live on that in Atlanta, Earl, let alone Chicago—especially on the North Shore. I've heard about the cost of living up here, and I've gotten a little taste of it during the last several weeks."

"I know that, but where else can you get a free apartment? And if we eat on the job, I'll pick that up too. I'll pay your car expenses, everything. And I'm not asking you to give up your free-lancing. What you do with your own time is your business. What do you say?"

I looked at Margo.

"Oh, no, you don't," she said. "Don't expect advice from me on this one. Sure, I'd love to have you a little closer to Pontiac, but it's still more than a hundred miles away. I'm doing what I have to do, and while it hurt me to do it, I decided without hearing from you. You're going to have to do the same."

"Can't you just tell me what you think?"

"Philip, only you know if what Earl is saying is true about your love for his kind of work. Could you supplement your income with illustrating? Would you enjoy working for him? Do you trust him? It's a big decision only you can make."

She was dead right as usual, but I wasn't about to decide right then. "How long can I have?" I asked.

"I'd like to know as soon as possible, but I won't push," Earl said. "I'll say this: I don't want there to be any mistake about it; we won't be business partners and we won't really be partners on the job either. We'll work a lot together, but I'll be in charge. You're no kid anymore, even though you're a novice at this. You'll be allowed all the usual mistakes, but only once. If you can't learn to avoid repeating errors, it won't work.

"I'm confident you can do it, but some day my life may depend on you, so I want it clear before you decide: you would be the subordinate, I would be the boss. You would be the student, I would be the teacher. You can speak your mind, but when I make a decision, it's a directive.

"Just like in the military, somebody's got to make the decisions because somebody is better, smarter, older, more knowledgeable, more worthy of leadership."

"And that's you," I said.

"You'd better believe it," he said. "And I don't want you thinking this would in any way be some cushy, fun job. You'd enjoy it, but you'd also learn what a grind it can be."

SEVEN

Mrs. Franklin didn't look like a woman who had spent her first night in jail. Petite and pretty, she looked ten years younger than she was. Margo and I were allowed to see her for fifteen minutes before her trip to Pontiac. All the former judge could talk about, it seemed, were the differences in life-style she would face.

"I will wear a denim jumper. Can you imagine? I haven't worn a jumper in nearly fifty years, and I don't ever remember wearing denim."

"You'll find it comfortable," Margo said lamely. Her mother nearly spit.

"You know, Margo, as a judge I toured Pontiac once. It was overcrowded *then,* and that was years ago. It had been spruced up for our visit, no doubt, but they couldn't disinfect everything. The stench still came through over the ammonia. I saw the dead eyes, heard the screams and catcalls. I got a view of prison life from that. Enough to know that I'm not capable of handling it."

Margo was startled. "What do you mean by that?"

"I will have no identity. No dignity. I will be stripped and showered and photographed and processed and quarantined. I will be segregated physically, of course, but unless I'm in solitary confinement—which would kill me—I'll still be able to see and hear the other women. It isn't that I don't know I deserve this. I've sentenced á lot of men and women to Pontiac, and even after visiting there I was convinced it was appropriate punishment. But I don't consider myself a hardened criminal. I won't be able to survive."

"Mother, you keep saying that. Can't you devise some plan of action, a way of keeping busy? Won't you have access to a library and study classes? And won't there be work to do?"

"Sure. I'll be working with the women I'm not allowed to live in the same cell with. Manual labor will certainly take my mind off my troubles, won't it? The first time a guard turns her back, I'll probably be killed.

"Reading and studying? What can they teach *me?* I could teach them. I've got a library at home to rival that of most law schools. What do you suppose will tempt me at the Pontiac prison library?"

Margo didn't respond. Her mother was rambling. And she was right. It would be horrible, especially at first. The contrast in life-styles could push her to the edge of suicide. She wanted comfort, but there was little Margo could say. You don't argue with a former lawyer and judge.

"I'll probably never see you again," Virginia said, lips trembling. "You, whom I have never loved the way I should and from whom I never accepted love, even though you tried hard. Do you love me, Margo?"

Her daughter nodded, unable to speak. "I will be alone," Mrs. Franklin said. "I won't survive."

"Nonsense, Mother," Margo managed. "You can have a visitor in three weeks. I'll be waiting by the door. And then I'll see you every week for as long as you want me to."

"You can't come that often."

"I can if I'm living in Pontiac."

"What?"

"I'm moving to Pontiac as soon as Philip can get me

back to Atlanta. I told you that you would always have me, Mother, and you will. I'll get a job and a place and I'll be there when you need me."

Mrs. Franklin stared at the floor. She shook her head slowly. "I don't understand you," she said. "You would do that for me? I can't ask you to do that. I can't let you."

Margo put her hand over her mother's. "You can't talk me out of it."

"Margo, you deserve a life of your own, don't you see? I've done enough damage. Don't make me live with the guilt of tying you down to a prison town in the middle of nowhere. I could be there a long time—if I live." Margo started to argue, but Mrs. Franklin cut her off. "You should be with Philip. You're right for each other. Please don't move to Pontiac, Margo. Please don't."

"Mother, frankly, it's good to hear you worrying about someone else for a change, and I don't mean that to be unkind. But I *will* be moving to Pontiac and I *will* be visiting you every time they'll let me. If you channel some of that caring attitude you just showed me, maybe you can help some of the women down there.

"Maybe you can teach a class on criminal law. Maybe you can even get better books into the library. Maybe you can work with the chaplain in helping counsel people."

"Wait, wait, wait," Mrs. Franklin said. "I've been impressed with you and your young man, and what your religious interest seems to have done in your life—"

"Mother, I've asked you not to call my faith in Christ 'religion.' It's not religion; it's a relationship with God."

"You lose me every time with that relationship business, as well as that 'it's not a practice, it's a person' double-talk. Anyway, it's working for you and you've certainly been kinder to me than seems humanly possible under the circumstances, but don't expect me to hook up with any chaplain or goody-two-shoes group in the hope that I'll get religion or God or whatever. Be encouraged that your old mom is impressed by you and Philip. And promise me that if you do settle in Pontiac, you won't think it entitles you to preach to me every week. If that's your motive, maybe you aren't so noble after all."

"Don't suspect my motives, Mother. I'm going to be there because I want to be and because you need me. You're in no position to be requiring promises from me. No, I won't preach to you, but I'm not saying I won't pray for you. And I'll give you things to read. If that library is as limited as you say, maybe some of the stuff Philip gave me to read will look appealing to you after a while."

"Will you write to me too?" Mrs. Franklin asked, switching emotional postures so fast I could hardly keep up.

"Of course I will, Mother. And I want you to stop berating yourself. You are paying for what you did, and whatever debt to me you feel is outstanding has been forgiven. You're paid up. You owe me nothing, and I will not be put off by you. You've got me whether you want me or not."

"I want you, Margo," Mrs. Franklin whispered, standing to embrace her daughter across the table. A Department of Corrections officer tapped on the door.

"One minute," he said.

"At least I don't have to ride all the way down there in a jail wagon," Mrs. Franklin said. "I get to ride in luxury in a Dodge station wagon." Margo tried to smile at her mother's attempt at levity, but she suddenly began to cry.

"You're going to get me crying too, Margo," her mother said. "It'll be all right."

"I'm supposed to be telling you that," Margo sobbed.

"Oh, don't buy this whole little-girl-lost bit of mine, honey. I'll survive because I'm a tough old bird and always have been."

Margo looked at me and we shook our heads. Was the woman crazy, or was this just her defense mechanism? A deputy entered and reached for Mrs. Franklin's arm.

"You don't need to touch me," she told him. "I'm perfectly capable of walking to the car." A matron put her hand on Mrs. Franklin's arm as she moved out the door. "Do you have to touch me?" Mrs. Franklin demanded, nearly shouting.

"No," the matron said meekly. And Mrs. Franklin walked in front of her, looking as much like a socialite out shopping as a murderer on her way to a twenty-five-year sentence in the state penitentiary.

Margo didn't speak for the first hour and a half of our drive to Atlanta. She faced the passenger-side door and laid her head on the seat back. She didn't move, but I knew she wasn't sleeping. She was crying.

"Anything I can say or do?" I asked. She shook her head.

I reached over and rested my hand on her knee. She covered it with her own and we rode in silence for miles. When her hand fell limp, I knew she had fallen asleep.

She didn't have much to say when we stopped to eat. I asked her if she wanted to drive. She didn't. I decided to drive straight through, hoping to reach Atlanta by midnight. "I'm going to need you to talk to me sometime this evening," I said.

"About what?"

"About anything, just to keep me awake."

She turned toward me and tucked her legs up under her. "I'm going to miss you, Philip," she said. "You don't think my decision to move to Pontiac was an easy one, do you?"

"I don't know," I admitted. "You never seemed to waver on it."

"I'm not saying I have any second thoughts about it. I just want to be sure you don't feel left out or hurt."

"I don't know what I feel."

"Understanding, I hope."

"I care about you," I said. "You know that."

"So does Earl Haymeyer," she said, "but he doesn't care where I live."

"He doesn't care for you the way I do."

"How do you care for me?" she teased.

"You know."

"You've never told me."

"I've never told you? You can't tell? Do you think all this has been the result of pity for you? If that's all it was, you've cost me several months of my life."

She grinned. "How much do I owe you?"

I pretended not to be amused.

"Philip, I'm only teasing you, don't you see? I just need to know where we stand. I'm confused and I don't want to presume anything."

"I am too."

"I hoped you wouldn't say that. One of us has to know what's going on here or we're headed for a dead end."

"I hope not."

"So do I, but Philip, if neither of us knows his own mind, how are we going to know what to do?"

"Maybe this separation will be good for us."

"That sounds familiar. Are you going to take the job with Earl?"

"Of course. I've never wanted anything so badly in my life. Except you."

"You want me?"

"You know I do."

"You've got me. When you can't stand being without me anymore, just write and tell my mother that you're coming to get me and that she'll be on her own after that."

"Be serious."

"OK, I'll be serious," she said. "If you wanted to work for Earl so badly, why didn't you tell him when he first suggested it?"

"You really want to know why? Because I was afraid you'd think I was being too hasty, frivolous, impulsive."

"Aren't you?"

"Probably."

"That's all right. I'm more impressed with the fact that you're worried about what I think of you."

"I have been for a long time."

"And I've never thought anything but the world of you for all that time," she said.

"But just out of gratefulness for my help, right?"

"No, I don't think so."

"Well, if we're so stuck on each other, how come we're both convinced that being apart is the right thing?"

"For one thing, we have little choice. I see no way around it unless I abandon my mother or you forget making a decent living."

"But is it fair that we can't be together, especially when we know we're right for each other?"

"Who said life was fair? God's ways haven't seemed entirely fair to me since I've become a Christian. He just does what He knows is right for me, and eventually I see that He was right from the beginning."

"And you put this in that category?" I asked. "God's will for us?"

"Since we have no choice, yes."

"What if we had a choice?"

"I hope we'd choose His way. This time He has made His way simple to find. We simply have no options. That gives me a certain sense of peace, even though I wish it could be different somehow."

"Margo, just what are we going to do if your mother's situation doesn't change for several years?"

"You'll become either a famous artist or a famous private detective who's independently wealthy and can make it anywhere."

"Even in Pontiac, Illinois?"

"Even in Pontiac."

EIGHT

We picked up Margo's car in Atlanta and moved out of our apartments. Three days later our two-car caravan pulled into Pontiac. I was towing a rented trailer with all our earthly belongings.

Finding a room for Margo was not difficult. The first ad we pursued was for the upstairs in the home of an old woman about a mile and a half from the prison. It included a bedroom, a bath, and a sitting room, plus some storage. It was perfect. Once we got her moved in I called Earl.

"How soon can I move to Glencoe?"

"How soon can you get here?" he said. "You're going to accept my offer then?"

"No, I was just curious," I deadpanned.

"Not funny," he said. "You can move in anytime you want. When'll it be?"

"Pretty soon," I said. "Margo's not even going to look for a job down here until she gets back from talking with Karlyn up there. We'll be heading that way soon."

A few hours later I got Margo checked into a North Shore hotel and then started moving my stuff into my new apartment. There was plenty of room for everything, including my drawing board. Earl then put Margo and me to work supervising the interior decorators who arranged the furniture and put the finishing touches on his offices while

Earl himself was tying up loose ends with Jim Hanlon. And he had been right; the sign on the door looked just right.

"So how did Hanlon take your resignation?" I asked later.

"Just like I thought he would. He wanted to know if it was final or if anything could change my mind. I told him a hundred thousand dollars a year might turn my head. He told me to leave my head right where it was. In fact, he said if I just checked in with him each day until April 1, he'd tell me whether or not he needed me. I guess things have really slowed down since your mother-in-law's trial."

"My mother-in-law? Not so fast, Earl."

"Tell me you didn't wish she was."

Margo pretended not to hear the conversation. She was more worried about Karlyn. "Can I call her early, as long as we're here?"

"I wouldn't," Earl said. "For one thing the EH Agency isn't geared up for any cases yet. Give us a few days. By a week from when you last called her, we'll be ready to really check this thing out. It'll be a good one for Philip to cut his teeth on. That reminds me. What do you two think of these?"

Earl fished around in a box of supplies for a brown paper bag from which he produced two square boxes. I slipped the top off one to find business cards inscribed with the EH Detective Agency name and phone number, and also "Philip Spence/Special Investigator."

"I ordered them the day after I talked to you, Philip. Just got 'em today. I'm glad you didn't turn me down after that kind of a cash investment in your future."

"What made you so sure?" I asked.

Haymeyer answered by asking Margo, "Did you have any doubt?"

"Nope."

"It was obvious in your eyes, Philip," Earl said. "And I'm glad to have you."

The phone rang. "Hello, yourself, Governor Hanlon," Haymeyer joked.

Margo and I wandered out and down the hall.

"I love you, Margo," I said suddenly. It just slipped out and brought her staring eyes right to mine. "I do," I said. She swallowed and said nothing.

When we returned, Earl was off the phone. "Do you suppose I could take Margo out to dinner tonight?" I asked him.

"Without me, you mean?" he shouted. "Girl, do you trust this man without a chaperone?" Margo laughed. "Of course, Philip," Earl continued. "Jim and I are meeting tonight anyway. In fact, why don't I just not see you two for a few days until we call Karlyn. My hunch is that Hanlon will officially let me go tonight. He's got a young guy he wants me to chat with, my heir apparent no doubt. Meanwhile, I'll see if anyone anywhere has anything on Karlyn May. There can't be too many people around with that name."

"Where will you look?" I asked.

"Everywhere. You'll find, Philip, that in our line of work we make a lot of friends, do a lot of favors, and are owed a few too. A bushel of buddies from the local PDs owe me a quick check of their microfilm files. I want to know anything at all about Karlyn May, a short, blue-eyed blonde, about twenty-five. That's all some of them will need to go on. If she had a parking ticket, a jaywalk warning, anything, I'll know about it by the time I see you again. I'll find out where she is taking her calls too. Have a good time."

As Earl headed for the door, Margo said, "PDs?"

"Tell her, Philip," he said. "She's gonna need a lot of teaching."

"Right," I said, as if I knew what he had meant by the initials. He left.

I looked at Margo sheepishly.

"So what did he mean?" she said.

"Uh, let's see. He said buddies at local PDs owe him stuff. And these people have some kinds of files—"

Haymeyer, who had obviously been listening at the door, popped his head back in. "Police departments," he said. "PDs. Don't forget to lock up, kid."

At dinner Margo teased me. "That was the first time you told me you loved me all by yourself."

"By myself?"

"Don't you remember? In the heat of the investigation of my mother you must have said something to Hanlon and Haymeyer about it because Earl said he thought you could get to mother because you loved me."

"Oh, yeah. And I've never told you myself until now?"

"Right."

"I'm sorry."

"That you love me?"

"You know what I mean."

"I told you first, remember?"

"I sure do."

"Do you really, Philip? Are you that romantic that you remember when I told you?"

"It's hard to forget. It was the only time."

"I still don't believe you remember."

"All right. It was a Sunday morning, before church, the day I would see your mother for the last time before her confession to the murder. We were in the suite between our hotel rooms."

"You're right as rain, inspector. I'm impressed."

"Must you always mock?"

"I'm not mocking, Philip. I'm impressed. I really am. And I'm sorry I haven't told you again since then, but I had a reason."

"And what was that?"

"I wasn't going to tell you twice before you told me once."

"That was a little childish, wasn't it?"

"Maybe, but why force myself upon you? I didn't know how you felt, except for that secondhand information once. I just didn't want to put any undue pressure on you."

"Loving me would put pressure on me?"

"If you didn't love me it would have, don't you think?"

"I suppose."

"You know, Philip, when I was a kid I loved romantic stories. I always have. But as I got into my last years of high school and beyond, I decided that love meant nothing. Family love had fallen apart. I didn't feel love for my mother, and sometimes I thought I pitied my father more than I loved him. And as for true love and all that, to me it was an illusion, a selfish feeling, a syrupy, self-serving fantasy. How could anyone know what love really was?"

"And now?"

"I still don't know *what* it is. I just know *that* it is, and it's real. And there are different levels of it. There was the unconditional love you felt for me when I was in trouble and wanting to kill myself. That was God-love. I know God is the author of all love. But this exciting, heart-pounding type of love that makes me want to look right into your eyes and tell you without embarrassment, that's the elusive love I never thought I would fall into."

"Aren't you afraid of analyzing it to the point where it becomes academic?"

"Do you want me to stop talking about it?"

"No, I don't," I said. "I get a kick out of your being so

straightforward and sure about it. It's not the way they talk about it in the movies, but it leaves me breathless just the same."

"You know what the best, the really best, part of it is, Philip? I mean, do you know how it is that I know this is the real thing and can be sure of it?"

"No, but I get the distinct impression that you're going to tell me."

"It's because as thrilled as I am to know that you love me—and I've known it at least as long as you have—I consider loving you even more of a privilege."

"I'm embarrassed."

"Don't flatter yourself, Philip. It's not because you're Prince Charming—though to me you are. It's just the way you let me love you. You don't drag it from me, beg me for it, play games with my emotions. You just let me show you, allow me to enjoy you, and you don't turn me away."

"Why would anyone ever want to do that?"

"You've seen it before, haven't you, Philip? I've had friends who dare each other to love them. They make it a psychological tug-of-war. We've been close to that when we've skirted the issue. I'm so glad it's out in the open now so I can just tell you. It excites me to just sit here and tell you to your face that your loving me is only icing on the cake. The cake is the privilege of loving you."

"I wish I'd said that."

"You have, many times. I waited to hear you say it out loud, but I haven't really doubted your love for a long, long time."

"I don't even know when it happened," I said. "Do you?"

"Not really. For me it might have been when I was holed up in Chicago in protective custody and you were out with Haymeyer and Hanlon trying to put the whole case together against Mother. You were so considerate of me and seemed eager to see me when you got back. I was miserable, yet I looked forward to being with you. All of a sudden I needed you, and not just for conversation. In fact, it scared me that I began to depend on you so much. That's when I started really evaluating my feelings. I didn't want a phony feeling of love just because you were all I had and because you had helped me through a crisis."

I didn't know what to say. I was flattered, thrilled, humbled. She was so sure of herself. "I always wanted to be an articulate suitor," I said. "I'll never be able to match you. Just know that I love you and that I hear you."

"I can't ask for more than that," she said.

NINE

One of the things I appreciated about Margo was that she rarely spoke seriously unless she had thought it all out first. And once it had been thought out, there was no stopping her. She'd give it to you with both barrels.

Margo had already figured out many mysteries of the Christian life that had eluded me as a "lifer" (a Christian since childhood) and explained them to me like a seminary student. And now she had explained her love for me and even mine for her. I had never met anyone like her, and I wasn't about to let her go now.

"I've come to a decision," she said.

"There's more?" I said.

"This separation is going to be rough on us, especially now that our feelings are out in the open. And you are the cause for that."

I shot her a double take.

"Well, Philip, if you hadn't said what you said, I wouldn't have said what I said tonight."

"You wouldn't?"

"Did you think I was just waiting for a chance to be alone with you before springing it on you? I could have told you all the way to Atlanta, couldn't I?"

"True enough. So what have you decided?"

"I've decided that if my feelings for you are real, then

true love means that I want the best for you, even if that means that I am not what's best for you. It would hurt, and I wouldn't understand it, but I would live with it."

"What in the world are you talking about?"

"I'm talking about being far apart, starting new lives. We'll meet new people. Our love might be diverted."

"I doubt it."

"I do too, and it's wonderful to hear you say that, but get my point: I will despair being without you, Philip. I will hate it. I will probably be tempted to forget staying close to Mother and just run to Chicago. But I won't do it. I won't worry that just because you're not in my grasp, or even in my sight, that I'm losing you."

"Well, you've got another one on me. That's exactly what I'll be worrying about."

"But here's the way I figure it—do you want to hear this?"

"Absolutely," I said.

"OK, if because of the distance and all the other factors I somehow lose you, even to someone else, I will rest in the fact that God wants only the best for you. If someone else is better for you than I am, then if I really love you and consider loving you a greater privilege than being loved by you, I will be able to accept it. I need to love you enough to be willing to let you go. And I do. I think."

I laughed. With that last "I think" she went from being the self-assured, articulate woman to the little girl who hoped she was right. "I'm glad you added that," I said. "I was beginning to feel like a commodity you were willing to sell or trade if it was best for the business."

"You weren't really, were you, Philip?"

"No. In fact, your thoughts are noble and beautiful. I love you, everything about you. Being loved by you is overwhelming. I guess I'm more selfish because I don't want to lose you. I wouldn't accept it. I wouldn't agree with God or anyone else that someone else would be better for you. Call it what you want, I'm not as Calvinistic as you are."

"Calvinistic? I knew I should have read everything you gave me."

"You read enough. A Calvinist is basically one who believes that what happens is what was supposed to happen. Let me tell you something in my own crude, nonromantic, slightly blue-collar, Dayton-versus-Winnetka way: No chance I'm going to lose you. I may not be as mature in my love for you as you are in yours for me, but then my expression of love was the one that slipped out suddenly. Yours had obviously been pondered for weeks."

"Months," she corrected.

"Church tomorrow?"

"I'd love it."

Earl Haymeyer had been right about Hanlon's wishes. He asked Earl to give a pep talk to the new man and then to feel free to get started on his own agency. On Monday morning, after he showed me where I'd land in the office, he told me to call Margo at her hotel and have her come in. "I want to brief you both on Karlyn May."

It was obvious that Earl was thrilled to have his own place. He strolled around the office in shirtsleeves, pinning notes to himself on corkboards all over the room. He had every piece of equipment and paraphernalia any police department detective squad room could have. Hardly anyone knew he was in business yet, and he had no idea if Karlyn May could pay for what he was willing to do for her, but he was ready. It was a case and he was working.

"The girl has no family," he told us. "She was orphaned at three and raised in a children's home in southern Michigan. She became a bit of an incorrigible and was transferred to a home for older girls in the Chicago area when she started high school.

"She went through a series of troublesome times, skipping school, shoplifting, generally raising cain with lots of boyfriends. Somewhere along the line she found religion."

"What do you mean by religion, Earl?" Margo asked. "Did she get involved in some cult or Eastern group, or did she become a Christian?"

"Well, girl, you see a difference there that I've never seen. In my mind, religion is religion. You've got yours and she's got hers. I couldn't tell you if hers is different or not, but I can tell you what group she got involved with."

It was a campus group Margo had never heard of, but I had. I smiled. "She's one of us," I told her. Earl looked puzzled, and I knew I hadn't done myself any good in planning future discussions with him on the subject.

"Whatever," he said. "She got involved with this group and became quite outspoken, had some sort of a conversion experience, and even went so far as joining in Christian outreach types of activities. My sources tell me she really changed. She had been a fringe student in a bad crowd and all of a sudden she threw that over for a nice appearance and a pleasant personality.

"Her grades improved, she was named to the homecoming court her senior year at Arlington High School, and she even spent a couple of years at a junior college in Palatine. She's held the same job for the last six years as public relations coordinator for a Des Plaines electronics firm. As best I can tell, she has told no one there or anywhere what's troubling her. Besides you, Margo. Still want to get involved?"

"We can't abandon her before we start," Margo said. "Anyway, if she's a Christian, we have a lot of common ground."

"Religion is all we need with her background to make her a real basket case," Earl said.

"If she's a Christian," Margo said forcefully, "she's got more than religion and it's the best thing for her."

Haymeyer raised both arms in surrender. "Whatever you say. I'm just thrilled that my first case might be a religious weirdo. I just wish I could start with a nice, clear-cut missing person or something."

"I hope you're not prejudiced against Karlyn already," Margo said.

"Let's try not to jump to conclusions, OK?" Haymeyer said.

"I won't if you won't," she said, smiling.

"Remember, at eleven we call her. She's taking the calls at a pay phone about three blocks from her apartment."

"How do you know all this stuff, Earl?" I asked.

"You'll learn, Philip, that with a name and a description, you can discover almost anything you want about anyone. Would you like to see the readouts on you and Margo?"

"You're kidding."

"Not at all. Here."

By giving our names and all the other information Haymeyer knew about us to his friends with access to the computers in the capitals of our respective states, he had come up with our social security numbers, educational records, employment, traffic and criminal records, and current crime-related activity. At the bottom of both was the notation: "Principal in the Virginia Franklin/Richard Wanmacher murder trial, Lake County, Illinois, March, 1990."

"I'd say we're up-to-date," I said.

"I'd say we're in a police state," Margo said.

TEN

Margo scared Karlyn May when she asked her on the phone if her boss at the Des Plaines electronics firm knew she was missing work because she was waiting in a phone booth for a call.

"How do you know where I am?" Karlyn asked.

"I know a lot more than that, Karlyn. I even know that you're a Christian."

Silence.

"Is it true, Karlyn? Are you?"

"Well, yes, but—"

"Did you know that Philip and I are too?"

Silence.

"Karlyn?"

"Are you?" Karlyn said. "Are you really? Tell me you are." She had begun to cry.

"We really are. Philip's an old pro. I'm a newcomer. But yes, we are."

"How does it feel to be an answer to prayer? I couldn't have hoped that the people I reached out to would be Christians. It was too much to ask. At first I wanted help from Christian acquaintances but I'm so scared and confused, I didn't know who to trust."

"You can trust me, Karlyn," Margo said, "and I'm going to ask you to trust me even further. I want you to meet me at Philip's apartment in Glencoe, and I want you to let me also bring our friend Earl. OK?"

"Who is this Earl?"

"I'll tell you when you come. You must trust us. Earl can probably help you more than Philip or I can, so I want him in on this from the beginning."

Karlyn hesitated. "I guess I have no choice."

"You have a choice, but I want you to choose to trust us."

Margo told Karlyn how to get to my place and encouraged her to put in a half-day's work before coming. "Meet us after dinner tonight, say at seven."

By late afternoon Earl was high from his first day at his own business. The secretary had gone home, we sat around trying to guess what Karlyn's problem was, and Earl ordered sandwiches from his favorite haunt. A delivery boy brought them at about six-thirty.

For as neat and trim as Earl is, he's the kind of a guy who can take a huge bite from a greasy burger with everything, stuff it into one side of his mouth, talk while he chews, and not gross you out. He's as articulate and quick while eating as when not.

"I'm guessing boyfriend problems," he said. "But it could be anything."

At about ten to seven a car pulled up outside. Earl stepped to the window and peered down. "I can't see who it is," he said, "but the driver isn't taking any chances. If it's Karlyn, she's worried she's been followed. She's just sitting there with the motor running, leaving herself lots of room to take off if someone pulls up."

"What do we do now?" Margo asked.

"You told her how to get in and up to Philip's apartment. Let's go and wait for her." Haymeyer swept the sandwich trash into the wastebasket, cut the lights in his office, and led the way down the hall. My apartment was on the same side of the building, so Haymeyer was able to watch Karlyn from there too. She stepped from her car while it was still running, looked in every direction, then reached back in to shut it off.

"It's her," Haymeyer said. "And she is a beauty, just like the tape showed."

She took the only entrance that led from the outside to the apartments and we heard her moving cautiously down the hall. Margo answered her knock. She seemed relieved to see Margo and greeted us all warmly, sounding a lot softer than she had on the phone.

"How can we help you?" Margo asked.

"First tell me about Earl, if you don't mind."

"There's no way around it," Margo said. "Right from the top you need to know he's a private investigator."

Karlyn stiffened and looked as if she felt betrayed. "You can trust him, Karlyn," I said, "if you can trust us. We value him as a friend and a professional. We trust him."

"I can't afford to pay anyone to help me," she said.

"I'm here unsolicited," Earl said. "If you ask more than I can give, I'll tell you."

"Thank you," Karlyn said. "I didn't expect this. I don't know what I expected. The only thing I do expect is that when I return to my apartment in Des Plaines tonight, no matter what time, someone will have been there."

"How do you mean?" Earl asked.

"I mean someone will have been there, just as someone has been in my apartment while I was at work or out anywhere for the last three weeks. Exactly twenty-one days."

"They wait for you?"

"No. They're never there when I arrive. They have simply been there."

"They make it obvious?"

"Not at first. About a month ago I first noticed that the

light in my hall closet was on when I hung up my coat at the end of the day. I couldn't remember having turned it on for anything. I complained to the management of the apartment complex that someone had been in spraying for bugs or cleaning the carpet or something and had left my light on. They assured me no one had been admitted to any of the apartments for months. I apologized, assuming I had been mistaken.

"A few days later my living room curtains were open. I always leave them shut during the day so people can't tell from the outside that no one's home. It makes for a depressing homecoming, but the first thing I do every afternoon is open them wide to the sun. That day I came into an apartment already warm and bright."

"And you figured you had forgotten again."

"No. That's one thing I don't forget because I pull the drapes shut every night before bed. I wouldn't be able to sleep if I thought someone could see through my living room window. There was no way I had opened those drapes before going to work. It's simply something I don't do."

"Did you complain to management again?"

"No, they had told me that they would inform me before they let in anyone for any reason. And if the maintenance staff had to get in, they were to leave a card so I'd know they'd been there."

"Is that all it's been?" Haymeyer asked. "Just something that could be attributed to a poor memory if someone wanted to be picky?"

"No, like I say, after those two episodes another few days went by, then I noticed a strange one. I have a certain way I hang my clothes. It's with the open side of the hanger hook pointing out. That means I put the clothes away by reaching in past the bar and hooking the hanger back toward me. I've done it since childhood. That afternoon I returned from work and noticed that two of my jackets were turned the wrong way in the front closet."

"Did you begin looking for little things like that all of a sudden?" I asked. "Is it possible that you had never really been that careful but that now these things jumped out at you because you expected them?"

"I know what you're driving at, but I don't think so. I'm weird that way. I do things a certain way and always have."

"So that was the third time something like that happened. How long was it before the next time you noticed anything?"

"The next day. The hangers were the first of three straight weeks of little messages. It's about to drive me nuts. I've had the locks changed. I've heard no noises, and no one has tried to get in at night. I've had friends stay over without telling them why, and no one has seen or heard anything they've told me about.

"When I'm alone I sleep with pots and pans near the windows so any intruder would make a lot of noise. I push furniture in front of the door to make it harder to get in. I even stayed in a motel one night so I could get a full night's rest. The next day a bottle of milk in my refrigerator was empty. I would never leave an empty bottle in the refrigerator. Anyway, I had just bought it.

"I began to leave notes for the intruder. I asked why he didn't just tell me what he wanted or leave me alone. The first note was ignored, I think, though my wall phone cord was looped up over the phone rather than hanging free the way I leave it. The second time, the note was folded in half and left right where I had written it."

Karlyn said she could hardly remember all the little things that had been changed in her apartment each day.

"It's never more than one thing," she said. "Am I crazy? I know I'm not imagining it."

"I'm not so sure," Haymeyer said. "I want you to know that. The phone cord, for instance. Couldn't a friend have used the phone and looped the cord without thinking? Was there some reason that made you start worrying about an intruder three weeks ago? Could your mind be playing tricks on you because you did something or said something that made someone upset with you?"

"Not that I know of. Believe me, there have been too many things like this for it to have been my imagination. There are things I haven't told you."

"Such as?"

"A poster turned around to face the wall. Why would I do a thing like that?"

"Do you think you did it?"

"Not while I was awake."

"Are you a sleepwalker?"

"No.

"One night my barbecue grill—which I haven't used since last summer—was full of charcoal, brand new coals from my previously unopened bag. The bag was stashed against the patio railings as usual, but it had been opened and used."

"And your apartment is on the second floor, right?"

"How did you know that?"

"From the number," Haymeyer said. "It starts with a two."

"What else do you know about me?"

"That you were under the care of a counseling psychologist for four years. Can you tell me what your basic problem was?"

"Well, it wasn't hallucinating, I'll tell you that. I wasn't insane or anything. I was a lonely, frustrated girl who never knew who her parents were, never felt loved, never felt accepted. My social worker said I had outgrown her when I received Christ and my life changed."

"I'd like to hear about that some time, Karlyn," Earl said. "But for now, did you happen to bring a change of clothes?"

"As a matter of fact, I did. What are you, a mind reader?"

"No, in fact I didn't figure that until I heard your story. No girl afraid of what she might find in her apartment during the light of day wants to go back alone to it in the middle of the night. Am I right?"

"You're right."

"Margo, can she stay with you at the hotel?"

"Well, she's certainly not staying here."

ELEVEN

"I hope we can get this solved before I leave for Pontiac again next week," Margo said the next morning. "I really like Karlyn and would hate to leave when this is only half done."

"Don't kid yourself," Earl said. "This could be a tough one. Luckily, right now it's all we've got to worry about. So let's worry about it. Did she say anything more last night?"

"She was pretty tired and the only things we talked about at the hotel were personal. Nothing of significance to the case, I would think."

"You don't know that, Margo. Everything in her life could be significant here. I need to know everything. Anything at all about her past or her work situation, anything."

"Well, she doesn't date much and has no real close friends. She's been involved in the same church for several years, but she likes the bigness of it and is not active other than attending regularly. People know who she is, of course, but she accepts few social invitations and while she has favorites among the people, there are none she would call personal friends."

"Strange," I said. "How could someone go to the same church for a long time without developing some friendships?"

"It may not be so strange to an orphan," Haymeyer said.

"Remember she was probably deeply hurt as a child. A person should have at least a few vague memories of early childhood, unless they are too painful to deal with. She probably felt abandoned and has always resisted close ties with people who might dump her later.

"Let's remember to ask her about childhood friends. What time did she get away this morning?"

"Fairly early. We stayed up late to talk, but she slept well and said she felt good. She's even prettier when she's rested, gentlemen."

"Then why didn't you bring her around to say good-bye?" I said.

"For that very reason. She did ask if we would meet her at her apartment after work today. I told her I'd call and let her know. Is it OK, Earl?"

"Sure, but I don't want it to be obvious that we're with her. If anyone is getting into her apartment only when she's gone, then her place is being watched. We want to be careful not to let the whole world know she has help all of a sudden."

"Earl," I said, "what do you mean 'if someone is getting into her apartment'? Do you doubt her story?"

"No, not at all. It's just that the mind can play funny tricks. Think back on all the things she said were clues that someone had been in her apartment. Any one of them could have been the result of a memory lapse, something else on her mind, whatever. All but the turned around poster, anyway."

"How do we find out if someone's been getting in?"

"That I'll show you tonight."

Margo spent her day writing a long letter to her mother and going to the library. Haymeyer taught me how to dust for fingerprints and put together a composite sketch of a suspect with various facial parts already drawn on overlapping sheets of acetate.

"I could draw them faster than this," I said.

"Then maybe you'll be even more valuable to me."

He also taught me how to handle a gun—not to shoot, but how to load and unload and clean it. "There's no such thing as an unloaded gun," he said.

"One more time?" I said.

"How many times have you read about kids, or even parents, who have shot someone—or even themselves—and were then quoted, 'I didn't know it was loaded'? If you treat the gun as if it's always loaded, you'll never fire it at anyone unless you intend to."

I was amazed to learn that he had never fired his gun in the line of duty in all his years as a detective. "To watch television, you'd think you guys are always shooting it out with someone."

"Nope, in fact I've pointed it at someone only a dozen times or so. The rule is, don't draw your gun unless you're prepared to use it, and don't fire unless you're shooting to kill. The only time you should ever draw it is to protect a life."

"I don't care to carry a gun," I said.

"That's probably just as well, Philip. Eventually you'll find it necessary, but for now you've got the right attitude. I don't get any thrill out of carrying one, but it sure evens the odds sometimes."

Haymeyer had a Polaroid camera with him when we left for Des Plaines in his new nondescript Ford station wagon. "I didn't want it to look like an unmarked squad car, but it couldn't be flashy either," he explained.

We waited in the parking lot of Karlyn's apartment

building until she returned from work. She acknowledged us with a tiny wave as she pulled in, but we did not respond. She had been instructed to leave the door ajar so we could just walk right in a few minutes later from another entrance.

Karlyn was in the living room looking for clues of the intruder when we walked in. Her deadbolt lock looked forbidding enough. "How could anyone get in here?" Margo asked.

"It wouldn't be easy," Haymeyer said. "The door could be popped with a simple tool in less time than it takes to open it with a key, but that deadbolt should be a deterrent to anyone but a pro, and even he would need time."

Karlyn led us to the bedroom, which was neat as a pin. She opened the closet. "Everything looks OK," she said. "Here and in the living room and the kitchen. That's eerie. That means whoever has been leaving messages for me the last three weeks knows I went for help."

"Don't assume too much," Haymeyer cautioned. "Have we seen everything?"

"All but the bathroom."

Karlyn walked past us from her bedroom and into the bathroom, but as we followed she turned and nearly bowled us over, terror in her eyes. "The shower curtain," she whispered. "Mr. Haymeyer, someone could be in the shower!"

Earl pushed us back into the hallway and asked Karlyn where the bathroom light switch was.

"On your right," she said, barely able to speak.

Earl took off his suit coat and laid it over a chair, drew his snub-nosed .38 with his right hand, and inched toward the bathroom.

Reaching across his body with his left hand, he switched

on the light and lunged toward the shower curtain, whipping it aside and dropping into a crouch, both hands on his revolver. "There's no one here," he said.

Karlyn was trembling. "You can say it's my memory or anything you want," she said, "but what girl living alone would close her shower curtain when she's not in the shower? I even check the closets before I go to bed to make sure no one's inside. If I left the shower curtain closed, I'd have to check behind it every time I walked by."

Margo nodded.

"How would you like to get out of here for a while, Karlyn?" Earl said.

"I would."

"Let's take a ride back up north so Margo can check out of her hotel. I'd like you to come back and stay with Karlyn until you have to leave for Pontiac, OK?"

"Are you kidding? I'm not so sure," Margo said.

"I'm not either," I said.

"You've never seen or heard this intruder. Right, Karlyn?" Haymeyer asked.

"Right."

"He comes only when you're gone and never at night?"

"So far—as far as I know."

"Then you two should be safe. Use your usual precautions, furniture against the door and all. For now, let's go back and get some dinner. Just let me shoot a few pictures first."

Haymeyer took two or three pictures in each room in an attempt to record things exactly as we left them. Then we were off, Margo and Karlyn in her car, Earl and I in his.

Dinner was nice. Karlyn was nervous and Margo wasn't much better. She was eager to help Karlyn, but she felt like a guinea pig, "or a sacrificial lamb," she said. The women weren't eager to head back to Des Plaines, so we chatted for a few hours until Haymeyer told them they'd better quit putting it off.

"Philip and I will wait in my office until we hear from you that you're in and safe and locked up."

"And alone," Margo said wryly.

"Yes," Earl said. "And alone."

Earl was showing me his photographic equipment that allowed him to make internegatives of Polaroid prints and enlarge them when the call came that would force him to do just that.

"I don't know what to make of it," Margo said, "but Karlyn insists that the thermostat has been tampered with."

"Oh, brother," Haymeyer said, "we're reaching a bit, aren't we? I'm getting just a bit dubious. Let me talk to her.

"Hello, Karlyn? Listen, what is different about the thermostat? You know how those things can always be off a degree or two. . . . Oh, it is? I see. Well, maybe there's a way I can check it. Meanwhile, get yourselves secured and try to get some sleep. You know where we are if you need us."

"What's up?"

"Karlyn says she never touches the thermostat. Two or three months ago she set it on automatic at sixty-eight degrees and never moved it. A little while after they got there, she noticed that the blower seemed to be running constantly, although the temperature seemed normal. She checked the thermostat and it was set at sixty-seven and manual."

"How do we determine if she adjusted it by accident or without thinking?"

"Come here. I'll show you. We can know for sure if anyone was in that apartment after we were."

TWELVE

It took Earl about an hour to make a huge enlargement of the tiny shot he had taken of the wall where Karlyn's thermostat was located. With a magnifying glass on a high contrast print, he could see that Karlyn had been right.

"When we left that apartment," he said, "the thermostat was set on sixty-eight and automatic."

"What now?"

"Sleep and then a stakeout. We'll find out just how sharp this bird is and if he knows when a place is being watched or not. We'll get there before Karlyn leaves for work and watch the place all day long. You're going to get a good idea of the occasional drudgery of this work. When we're not staring at parking lots and entrances and comings and goings, we'll be running for coffee, covering each other for catnaps, and interviewing people in the building about whether they've seen anything at all."

"Sounds like a drag," I said.

But it wasn't. I rather enjoyed showing people my new business card and asking if I could speak with them a moment. Few wanted to talk at first, assuming that I was trying to sell something. There was not a person on Karlyn's floor who didn't know who she was, though most had never spoken to her. Almost all referred to her in some variation of "that beautiful, quiet, little blonde."

No one had seen anyone coming or going from the apartment when Karlyn wasn't home, though most had noticed two men and a woman who entered after she did the afternoon before.

"I'm completely baffled," I admitted to Earl. "I suppose you've got it all figured out."

"No, but I'm not ready to throw in the towel yet. I can't admit I'm stumped, even if it's true. It might make a bad impression on you. But what did I tell you about perseverance? Somebody knows something, and we're gonna find out who it is."

With Margo in the apartment virtually all day every day, there was enough activity to scare off any intruder. But that made it obvious that the place was being watched. As long as someone was there, no attempt was made to leave "messages." We learned nothing by interviewing more people in the building. A week passed and Margo began making plans to leave for Pontiac.

"I hate to do this to you, Karlyn," she said. "But I have no choice."

"I understand. But I'm sure going to miss you and all the time we spent talking and praying and reading."

"Yeah," Margo said, "and watching TV and cooking and eating. It's been fun in spite of the circumstances."

"I guess Philip will just have to take over where Margo left off," Haymeyer said.

"Fat chance," Margo said, throwing a pillow at him.

"Seriously, I am about to turn this case over to Philip," Earl said. "I'm getting more and more business as my old contacts discover that I'm available. We need some hard legwork done before we get a real lead, and that's what you're here for, Philip."

I couldn't deny I was excited, but I told Earl I would need his counsel.

"I'll be around," he said. "Nothing I have lined up will take me out of town. You can talk to me anytime you want, but as of tomorrow morning, this one is yours."

"How do you feel about that, Karlyn?" I asked. "You sought out Margo, got Earl instead, and now I'm subbing for him."

"I'd feel guilty if I didn't tell you I'd rather have Earl on it, but if he feels you can handle it, who am I to say you can't? I can't pay either of you, so I appreciate any help I can get from anyone. Don't get me wrong. You're the one who helped Margo when she needed it, so you've got that experience."

"The cases are hardly similar," I said.

"And let's not let the consequences be similar either," Margo said, smiling.

Margo was more talkative than usual as we loaded her car the next morning. She was concerned about everything from the fact that she hadn't heard from her mother by phone or letter to what she should wear the first time she visited. "What does one wear to a prison?" she asked.

She double-checked that she had everything and slid behind the wheel. I got in the other side just to sit with her for a minute. She finally ran out of nervous energy and turned in the seat to face me.

"So—" she said.

"So," I said.

"So now you're a private eye."

I winced. She didn't want to be serious. "Yeah," I said, "and someday I'm gonna track you down." She leaned over and laid her head against my chest. I smoothed back her hair.

"This is not going to be easy," she said softly.

"Hm?"

"Leaving you."

"I know."

"I mean I knew it was coming, but I thought I'd be ready. I'm not ready, Philip."

"Neither am I."

"But we're not kids; we have no choices, do we?"

"No, Margo, we don't."

"I mean, if we were high school kids, I could just forget this trip. You could skip school. We could spend the day in a park somewhere and get yelled at when we got home. And maybe grounded."

"Those were the good old days," I agreed. "Only in Dayton there wasn't anything worth skipping school for."

"There was in Winnetka, only I was never invited."

"Skip school with me, love. Forget Pontiac and I'll forget my responsibilities to Earl and Karlyn. What do you say?"

"I say you're as crazy as I am."

"Just crazy about you, Margo."

"My, what a quick wit and tongue! How do you come up with 'em so fast? You should be in the movies!"

"You really know how to hurt a guy. You set me up for that dumb retort, you know."

"But I had no idea you'd just jump right in there with 'crazy about you'!"

"Oh, be quiet. I don't know if I'll ever survive your mockery."

"Here's hoping you get plenty of time to find out."

"You'd better get going," I said, looking at my watch. Margo looked up at me. I leaned down and kissed her.

"Oh, to be a kid again," she said. "I swear I'd forget this trip."

"You are a kid. Now get going." I jumped out and ran around to her window.

"There are so many things I want to say," she said. I put my finger to her lips.

"Call me when you get there," I said. "Write me often. Let me know when you can come up, and make it soon." I took my hand away.

"Parting is such sweet sorrow," she said. "More sorrow than sweet." And she pulled away.

I'm not one who waves to cars as they fade from sight, so I just got in my car and headed for Des Plaines. I tried to think about whether it would be right to get Karlyn's permission to tell her employer or the police or the apartment complex management what was going on. I decided I'd better check with Haymeyer first, but it was hard to keep my mind on the case.

All I could think of was how little time I had spent alone with Margo since returning from Atlanta. I missed her already and didn't need that while trying to make heads or tails of my first investigation. I called Earl.

"No, Philip. No police yet. Let me deliver the intruder to them when the time comes, unless we need them. And let's not say anything to the apartment managers because I haven't ruled out the possibility that they could be involved somehow. How else is someone getting into that place without force and without being noticed? As for her employer, that's entirely up to her."

Karlyn agreed to meet me for lunch, where I gingerly broached the subject of telling her employer what was going on. "It can only help you," I said. "Earl discovered that the personnel department is already worried about you."

"But what if it's someone there?" she said. "The word will get out and whoever is doing it will change tactics."

"Do you have any reason to believe it might be someone from work?"

"I don't have any reason to believe anything anymore," she said. "I've racked my brain to think of anything I've said or done to anyone that would prompt them to torment me like this. I scribbled a list of everything I could think of in the last year. I don't know what good it will do you, but you can see it if you want."

"Sure," I said, and read it as I ate. Karlyn picked at her food. She had listed a minor traffic accident she had caused the previous winter.

"I didn't know how to report it or even if I had to," she said. "I thought the police report would go to my insurance company or something. I didn't mean to be so dumb. After about six months I got a letter from the guy I hit asking me to please inform my insurance company so he could get his car fixed. I did that, but a few months ago I heard from him again. My insurance company had contacted him, but no settlement had been made yet. He wasn't too happy, but he seemed like a nice enough guy. Worth checking out?"

"Of course," I said.

THIRTEEN

"Don't waste too much time on this insurance claim thing," Haymeyer warned me. "I ran across the same incident when I was checking her out. The guy is from out of state. All you need to do is verify that he's not been in Illinois during the last month and you can rule him out. It's pretty thin soup anyway, thinking that a victim of a fender bender would try to scare a girl to death."

"Makes sense, I guess," I said. "How many of the leads that sound good to me are going to become dead ends?"

"All but the last one."

"Very funny."

"Just hang in there, Philip, and don't expect it to be easy. Very, very often the tip that leads you to the answer will seem like coincidence or stroke of luck."

"But it isn't?"

"Of course it isn't. It would be luck only if you had it drop in your lap when you weren't doing your homework. If you're working hard you make your breaks. It's just like in sports. Doesn't it always seem like the team that gets the breaks wins?"

"Yeah."

"Think about it. It's really the other way around. The winner, the champion, the hustler is in a position to get the breaks. He makes the breaks. You may be looking in one direction and have something pop up in another, but you wouldn't know it if it slapped you in the face unless you were looking just the same."

"I'm not sure I follow, but I'm stubborn enough to stay on this."

"That's all it takes."

"I hope you're right. Is there anything else you ran across that I should know about so we don't duplicate efforts?"

"I'm sorry I didn't give you Karlyn's readout. I'll have it for you tonight."

"Say, Earl, this may sound weird, but do you ever just stop and think about a case? I feel I need to do that, but I feel guilty if I'm not driving around, talking to Karlyn, or trying to track something down. I need noodling time, or at least I feel I do."

"Exactly right, Philip. Remember when you and Jim Hanlon and I used to sit around with the other agents and maybe Larry Shipman and just brainstorm? Sometimes it lasted an hour or two, and we would just try to get inside someone's head and decide what we would do if we were him?"

"Yeah."

"Well, if you really hit a dead end, just drive to the beach and think the thing through."

"I'd probably wind up thinking about Margo."

"Then track down Larry Shipman. It'll be good experience for you because that's a job for any detective. No one ever knows where he is. Find him and see if he'll spend some time discussing the case. He knows nothing of it yet, so tell him and swear him to secrecy. In telling him maybe something will break loose in your own mind. You may find him a step ahead of you, though. He's a thinker."

Shipman's phone-answering device told me that Larry was either sleeping or gone and that if I called again right away and he was sleeping, he'd wake up and answer, but that if I was a burglar and that didn't work, not to assume he was really gone or I'd risk getting my head blown off when I broke into his apartment. A really different kind of a guy.

I called back right away and got the same message, so I went to his place in downtown Chicago and banged long and hard on his door.

A neighbor told me he had seen Larry leave about an hour before, but the neighbor had no idea where he was headed. "You can bet it's either to the paper, the radio station, the TV station, or—"

"Or what?"

"Or the police department. You never know."

I called all those places. He had been to each, except for his favorite radio station, so I figured he was making the rounds of his haunts. They didn't expect him, but then they never expected him. I drove over and asked for him. "He hasn't been here," the girl said. Intuition told me to wait in the parking lot.

Intuition was right. I was encouraged. Maybe I could be a detective after all.

"Philip, my man, how ya doin'?" Larry said as he breezed into the studio. "You and Happy Haymeyer get that blonde caper settled yet?"

"No, and that's why I'm here. I'd like to bounce some ideas off you if you have the time."

"What'll it take?"

"Maybe an hour."

"Sure. Is this a freebie?"

" 'Fraid so."

"That's OK, Philip. I made a few skins off your future mother-in-law's case. I can give you an hour as soon as I'm through here. C'mon with me."

I followed him to the news director's office and listened as he played a few cassette recordings he had made just that morning. One was an interview with a fireman at the scene of a fatal fire. The other was with the mother of a hit-and-run victim.

"This is dynamite stuff, Larry," the news director said. "I don't know how you do it."

"It's all because of the praise and glory and money, and because of my little scanner radio that tells me where the cops are at all times."

"We've got the same radios, Larry, but even when we beat you to the scene, we don't get the interviews you get. That's what makes you our best stringer."

"That's music to my ears, but I bet you tell that to all the brilliant people you meet. Just wait till you find out that I use actors and make these things up."

"You'll be hearing from me soon," the newsman said.

"Hey, I haven't heard from you yet on last week's stuff."

"Are you serious?"

"Yeah."

"Larry, I'm sorry. You know we're usually pretty tidy on these things, especially with you. I'll call accounting right now and get it in the mail to you tomorrow."

"A likely story." Shipman laughed, tossing the man the untouched half of a roast beef sandwich. "We'll be talkin' to ya."

Larry is a constant mover, always on the go. He swept past me and was down the hall and out the door to the parking lot before I had hardly begun to move. He held the door open for me and then clapped, rubbed his hands together, and said, "Philip, let's talk blondes."

He directed me to a deserted Lake Michigan beach where frigid waves lapped not far from the car. "I want to hear it all, and you've got an hour of my prime time." He was dead serious and stared straight into my eyes for the twenty minutes or so it took me to tell Karlyn's story.

Shipman looked dubious about all the clues, especially after I said she had changed the lock. I concluded, "So Earl determined that someone for sure had been there by blowing up the picture of the thermostat and showing the different setting."

Shipman lowered his eyes and sat gazing at the dashboard. "Let's walk," he said and was quickly out of the car and down the beach. I ran to catch up. He said nothing for a long time but just ran his hands through his hair and kept moving. Finally he stopped and looked around, as if the answer had just whizzed by and he had nearly missed it. "I want to see her place," he said abruptly.

"It's nearly time for her to be off work, and my hour with you is almost up," I said.

"Hey," he said, "did I ask for anything? No self-respecting journalist can ignore a real mystery. Just let me see her place."

We got there just a few minutes before Karlyn was due home from work. "I don't want to be here when she gets here," he said. "Let me just check it out quickly."

We went to her apartment and rang the bell, not expecting any answer, of course. But while I stood there, shielding anyone's view of Larry, he popped the door lock and nearly jimmied the deadbolt. "I could have been in in another minute or so," he said. "But then I know what I'm doing. No way anyone could have gotten in there fast enough to not be noticed. Not every day for three straight weeks anyway."

We went down and out and around to the back where

Larry leaped from behind some bushes on a dirt incline and caught hold of the railing on Karlyn's patio. He pulled himself onto the ledge and climbed over the rail.

"Notice anything?" he called out.

"No, I can't even see you."

"Move over to where I jumped up from."

"I still can't see you."

"Move to your left about three feet and crouch. Now can you see me through the bushes and the railing?"

"Just barely."

"Then you noticed what I wanted you to notice."

"No, I didn't. I can hardly see you."

"That's what I wanted you to notice. Now if you can get up here, I'll show what else you can't see."

It wasn't difficult, even though I am not as athletic as Larry. "Now look," he said. "Can you see anyone else's patio?"

"No, that's neat how they designed these for privacy, isn't it?"

"Ducky," he said. "Don't you see, Philip? If you can get around behind the building with no one seeing you, you can get onto the second floor patios without trouble. And once you're on the patio, no one can see you. Do you have any idea how easy these patio sliding doors are to open?"

"No, but you're going to show me, aren't you?"

Shipman placed both hands, palms out, on one of the glass doors, leaned in, and lifted. The entire side was freed from the bottom track. He could have lifted it out, but we heard the lock being turned from the hallway door.

"Karlyn's home," I whispered. "Let's get out of here before we scare her to death!"

We nearly knocked each other down trying to get to the railing, but Shipman got there first, neatly planted one hand and catapulted himself over the side into the bushes. The door clicked from inside. Another second and Karlyn would have a clear view of my silhouette on the curtain. I tried to do what Shipman had done but chickened out of letting go in mid-air and found myself hanging from the other side of the railing. As the front door opened, I let my hands slide down the rail until I hung out of sight from the concrete patio floor.

I hung there with scraped wrists and aching fingers, but Shipman was no help. He was trying so hard not to laugh that he was nearly crying, hiding his eyes.

"Hang in there," he whispered, causing himself to laugh even more. "I'm comin' to get ya, Tarzan!" He grabbed my ankles just as I heard footsteps inside and let go of the ledge. With Shipman holding my ankles, I hit the dirt incline headfirst, and we both bounced into the bushes.

We were like a couple of drunken sailors staggering out of there, I rubbing everything that hurt, Shipman trying to control his laughter.

"You're lucky I'm free tonight," he said in the car. "Let's see if we can get some time with Earl. The only thing better than this is hearing me tell about it." I was only slightly amused.

Haymeyer could hardly contain himself. "Are you hurt, Sherlock?" he asked.

"No, but I wish I was. I'd have something to show for my heroics."

"Well, did you boys come up with any leads, or did you just spend the whole afternoon monkeying around?"

"Boo," Shipman said.

"I learned that whoever is doing this is doing it from the back," I said.

Haymeyer and Shipman broke into mock applause. "Very good, Philip," Earl said. "Have mercy, Larry. The kid's gonna make it yet!"

"I can't win," I said.

"Seriously, Earl," Shipman said. "I do think there is one part of Karlyn's history that deserves our attention."

FOURTEEN

Earl and I looked at each other as if to ask if Larry was being serious. "We're ready," Haymeyer said.

"The orphanage," Shipman announced. "Philip, how big are you?"

"About five ten and a hundred seventy-five pounds."

Haymeyer and Shipman rolled their collective eyes. "Philip, you are talking to trained observers," Haymeyer scolded. "I don't suppose you'll get in trouble with your church for exaggerating a bit, but at least tell us the truth. There's no way you're taller than five nine, and it'll be years before you see a hundred seventy-five pounds."

"OK," I said, "I'm five eight-and-a-half and a hundred sixty-four."

"What does all this have to do with the orphanage?" Earl said.

"My theory is this, gentlemen: a woman could get onto that patio just as easily as we did today."

"I'll grant you the physical part of it," Haymeyer said, "but is it logical? Is there anything else that says our man is a woman?"

"Cute," Shipman said. "And yes, there is, if Philip got the story straight. Think about it. There have been no threats. No notes, no breathy, wordless phone calls. No weapons. Just irritations. Little things done a different way. Little things that only a woman might know would bother another woman."

"But why would this female enemy have to come from the orphanage? Why not the girls' school? Or high school? Or from work?"

"It's just a guess. Hurts inflicted at childhood are the deepest and most painful, aren't they?"

"I don't know, Dr. Freud. I'm just a flatfoot."

We all sat thinking about it. Finally Earl spoke again. "The scariest messages for Karlyn were the shower curtain and the folded note, but that was only because the one hinted at an ambush and the other seemed to be a direct answer to a communication. You may be onto something, Larry."

"Should we get Karlyn in on this discussion?" I asked.

"No, I'd sooner get Margo's ideas. I don't want Karlyn trying to figure out which girl she knew in the orphanage might be visiting her apartment every day, when we're only guessing ourselves. Ask Margo when she calls, will you, Philip?"

Margo's drive south had been uneventful. "Tomorrow I'll be beating the bushes for work," she said. "I miss you already."

"I missed you first," I said.

"Don't be too sure. Philip, I really need to ask you something serious, if you have a few minutes."

"I have something serious to ask you, too, if you have the rest of your life."

"Really, Philip. I need your help."

"OK, I'm sorry."

"It's about Mother. I got my first note from her. She says she feels vulnerable there. Isn't that weird? Why should she feel vulnerable when she's separated from the other inmates?"

"I don't know. Maybe it's paranoia. After so many years in a position of power, now she's a nobody and she doesn't like it. What do you make of it, Margo?"

"I think she might be ready for a real spiritual push. I'm tired of trying nudges."

"I hadn't thought of it that way, but maybe."

"What do you think about my explaining all about why I became a believer in Christ? In a letter I mean, so she won't interrupt me or act embarrassed as usual. And then I'll tell her we can discuss it when I see her or when she's ready."

"With that analytical mind of hers, that may be the best. You might do better on paper too."

"You know I've tried several times in person. I guess I'm just too emotional. I've never been able to talk her into anything either, and I'm still intimidated after all these years. I'm eager to get something down and off to her soon. I'll be seeing her in a week or so, you know. I do need some advice first though."

"Like what?"

"Like what I should write."

"Hit me with what you had in mind."

"She already knows what I feel Christ has done for me, but my needs are not her needs. What do I tell her, Philip? I want to start with the fact that the Bible says she's a sinner and lost and that she needs Christ to assure herself of eternal life. I just don't know how she'd respond."

"I don't either. For sure she knows she's done wrong. She's lived with that for years. Maybe you should emphasize that Christ offers her abundant life. You'll find that in John 10, specifically verse 10. And convince her that she can be free, even in prison. John 8:32 says that she can know the truth and that the truth will set her free."

Margo was silent.

I continued. "She needs to know that Christ's death paid for her freedom and that if she would give Him a chance to change her life, she might eventually adopt John the Baptist's philosophy in John 3:30. That would be the full cycle for her, Margo. From being the god of her own life for more than fifty years to getting out of the way so Christ can take over."

"That would really be something, Philip. That really would. What you're telling me is that if I know the book of John, I can write the letter I need. Maybe what I should do is read the book through a couple of times first."

"As long as you're going to do that, try it in a couple of different versions."

"Great idea. Thanks, Philip."

"Now, let me pick *your* brain for a minute."

"Sure."

I asked her what one little girl could do to another that would make her hate the first so much that she would harass her like Karlyn was being harassed.

"I'd have to think about that one," she said. "I don't have any experience with orphanages, but I imagine they can be pretty rough. Can you find out if there were boys there? That can lead to some knock-down, drag-out fights sometimes. But I suppose Earl is looking for evidence of a quarrel that was never resolved by a fight."

"I suppose."

"I'm sorry, Philip. I'll keep thinking about it, but that's all I can come up with right now."

Haymeyer and Shipman agreed that Margo was probably right about the unresolved quarrel. "But we want to be sure we aren't going off the deep end on the wrong idea," Earl said. "It's easy to build a case on a theory and then find out the theory itself is wrong."

"How often have *my* theories been wrong?" Shipman asked. "Don't answer that."

"You were sure right about Olga Yakovich giving the Wanmacher murder weapon to her son," Earl said.

"Yeah, but I was a few hours too late with that brainstorm, wasn't I?"

We were silent for a few minutes, reliving in our minds the horror of finding the body of that slim, young college kid on the floor of his room, a gaping wound where his throat had been slit.

"I'm not sure I'm cut out for this kind of work after all, Earl," I said. "I dread being too late in finding out who's playing games with Karlyn. If we found her injured or worse, I'd never forgive myself."

"You have to forgive yourself sometimes, Philip," Shipman said. "I could blame myself for Jon Yakovich's death if I thought it was my responsibility to think like a criminal before the criminals do. But there was nothing I could have done about it. We raced over there as soon as we thought of it, but he had been dead several hours. What could I have done?"

"I just don't want us to be sitting around trying to think of motives and suspects while Karlyn might be already hurt," I said.

"Nobody's disputing that, Philip, and maybe that's why you are cut out for this business. You've got to care. If you don't, you'd just wait for the murders and then enjoy figuring out whodunit. That's not for me."

"Me either," I said.

"Then let's go to work," Shipman said. "I'm still trying to figure out why Earl, the best gumshoe in the state, and I, upon whom the entire city of Chicago depends for its news, are spending all this time helping an apprentice investigator with his first case, and for no bucks."

"I do appreciate it, guys. You know that, don't you?"

"What have you done for me lately?" Shipman asked.

"I gave you a good laugh in the bushes and don't you forget it."

"I couldn't if I tried, believe me."

"Let's call Karlyn," Earl said.

She was eager to have us visit her, though she was a little nervous when Larry showed up too. Again we had to convince her that he was more than just another person getting involved.

Today's clue had been the bed covers turned back, the way it's done in nice hotels. "Fits my theory," Larry said, piquing Karlyn's curiosity.

"Which is?" she said.

Shipman looked to Earl for permission.

Earl nodded. "But first let me explain our new tactics. From now on we don't try to pretend we don't know someone has been here. We don't try to hide that we're looking for the person. I think the suspect wants to be caught because otherwise he or she would have tried something more severe. There's something darkly symbolic about the bed covers being turned back, and I don't like it. Could mean we're heading toward a confrontation. It would be nice to know who we're dealing with before that happens."

Karlyn looked sick. "I'm not sure I like what I just heard," she said.

Haymeyer leaned forward and rested his elbows on his knees. "I'm not trying to be tough on you, Karlyn, but welcome to the adult world. This is happening to you, so I'm through talking in circles about it as if it concerns someone else. You're being hassled and threatened and it scares you, I know. But you can't avoid the truth just because you don't like how it sounds. Keep your wits about you and stay with us. Don't hide behind us. Lead us to your pursuer."

"I don't have any idea who he might be!"

"Go ahead, Larry. Hit her with your idea."

Karlyn was fascinated and tried to rack her brain for memories of childhood battles. "There were many," she said. "Which one would lead to something like this?"

"Something unresolved."

"That was the one good thing about the home in Kalamazoo," she said. "For as strict as the matrons were, they didn't allow fighting and arguing to go unfinished. There was a complete airing of the problem and someone was always punished—"

Karlyn stopped and appeared to be deep in thought. "There was a girl," she said, "whom I liked so much that I wished she were my mother. She was only a couple of years older than I was, but she was a true friend."

"We need someone who wasn't necessarily a friend," Shipman said.

"Well, something happened with us," Karlyn said. "And she quit being my friend."

"Tell us all you can about her and the situation," Earl said, "and Philip will take notes."

Karlyn folded her hands in her lap and looked down. "I was six," she said carefully. "LaDonna was eight. LaDonna Finch. I thought she was the most beautiful girl in the world. I couldn't believe that she liked me too. We played together every chance we got, but we had to work too. From age four on up everyone had specific duties and were punished if they didn't do them.

"LaDonna always talked about her parents coming back for her some day. No one believed her because most of us didn't have parents, and those who did were not often visited by them. But LaDonna, the girl with the beautiful name, did. Her mother came about every six months and promised it would be only a little while longer before she would take her home again and she would meet a new daddy.

"It was a promise most of us had heard her recount so many times that many had stopped believing it. But I didn't. I wanted it to be true for LaDonna, but I didn't want her to leave either. She never knew how much I needed her to be my friend and protector. She stuck up for me all the time. That's probably why she never understood why I didn't stand up for her."

"You let her down?"

"Not intentionally. I could have saved her from a paddling if I had been more forceful. We were supposed to clean up the television room before visiting hours and we were not allowed to leave until it was done. She and I were nearly finished when she saw her mother's car pull up. 'Oh, please finish up for me, Karlyn,' she begged. I said, 'Sure, LaDonna.'"

Karlyn looked up at us.

"She got in trouble for that?" Shipman asked.

"Miss Kepkey came in just a few minutes later and demanded to know who was supposed to be helping me. I said, 'LaDonna, but—' and I was going to tell her that I had said I would finish up.

"'I'll teach her for leaving all this work to you,' she said, and before I could say anything more, she left. I got to meet Mrs. Finch that day. LaDonna's mother had the same jet black hair cut in a pageboy that LaDonna had. She seemed so nice, nothing like I thought a mother would be like who left her daughter in an orphanage.

"While we were talking, Miss Kepkey interrupted and told LaDonna that she wanted to see her in her room as soon as visiting hours were over. Mrs. Finch asked if anything was wrong, and Miss Kepkey just said, 'Nothing that can't be handled.' Then she looked at me and walked away.

I had a stomachache for days every time I thought of that look."

"So what happened?"

"When Mrs. Finch left, LaDonna went back to her room. I followed her but waited outside the door because I knew Miss Kepkey was in there waiting for her. 'Well, aren't we just something?' she said to LaDonna. 'A pretty, black-haired girl and her rich, black-haired mama all gussied up and wonderful? And you think that entitles you to leave little Karlyn to do all the work?'

"LaDonna started to protest but Miss Kepkey told her, 'Karlyn told me how you left her with the whole job! Now bend over!' LaDonna started crying and saying it wasn't true, that I had said it was OK, but Miss Kepkey kept yelling at her to bend over."

Karlyn buried her head in her hands and wept. "I'm sorry. I haven't thought about this in years."

"Take your time," Earl said. "I really think we might be onto something here."

"Well, Miss Kepkey smacked LaDonna's bare skin with the paddle so hard and so many times that LaDonna screamed and screamed. I wanted to run away but I was frozen. Suddenly LaDonna stopped screaming and I heard her tumble to the floor. Miss Kepkey kept insisting that she get up, but LaDonna wasn't moving.

"I ran to the headmistress and said, 'She's hurt LaDonna bad, she's hurt her so bad!' and I pointed down the hall. Mrs. Miller ran into the room just as Miss Kepkey was coming out, the paddle still in her hand. Mrs. Miller screamed when she saw LaDonna."

FIFTEEN

"Just relax for now," Haymeyer said. "When you're ready, tell us whatever else you can about the incident."

"I'm all right," Karlyn said. "I can tell you. That was the worst, but things were never the same between LaDonna and me. She was never mean—she never had been—in fact, I don't think she had a mean streak in her." Haymeyer and Shipman caught each other's eye as if to say, *I'll bet*.

"Did LaDonna try to get back at you?"

"She never said one word to me for the last year she stayed there. Nothing, Not one word. I could hardly stand it. I cried and begged her to say hi to me, to hit me, to kick me, to yell at me, to take my toys, anything. I wanted her to acknowledge that I existed. She would come into a room and merely look at me. I'd smile, say something, or hand her something, and she would ignore me as if I weren't there. She kept it up longer than I ever would have been able to.

"I tried to tell her what had happened, that I hadn't really told on her, but she walked away. I followed her around, asking if she understood and if it was OK now. She never said another word to me."

"Did she speak to other girls?"

"Yes, but she was not the same girl she had been. She had been the happiest, cheeriest girl in the place, but now she was subdued. She was in infirmary for two weeks and her seat was tender for another two.

"I've not had a real friend since. I blame myself for losing LaDonna, even though down deep I know it wasn't my fault. I tried to make it right with her, but she just wouldn't listen. I think she was hurt even more deeply than I was. It could be that she never got over it. But she wouldn't be doing this to me now. It wouldn't make sense."

"Well," Shipman said, flopping back in his chair, "think what you want. I'd say you've got a possibility here. This is the very way deep-seated hostilities come out after many years."

"But nineteen years?" I asked.

"Why not? It depends on how deeply LaDonna's mind may have been scarred."

"Bizarre."

"For sure," Haymeyer said. "And you'd better check it out."

"Where do I start?"

"At the Creekside Home for Girls, Kalamazoo, Michigan, I guess."

"They won't tell you anything," Karlyn said. "At least they never told me anything."

"You tried to look up LaDonna?"

"No, my parents."

"Well, that's different. In fact, they'd probably have to give you that information now too, with the new laws. It's worth checking out. Maybe Philip can go there and ask about that."

"You know what?" Karlyn said. "If you find out it could be LaDonna, I don't even want to know. I just want to go where she can't find me. I was almost to the point where I was over that hurt. But now this. I still can't believe she's got it in her."

"Karlyn," Haymeyer said, "you read about Margo and Philip in the paper, right?"

"Right."

"Can you imagine what it must have been like for Margo to live with the knowledge that her mother was a murderer?"

"No, I can't."

"But what's worse, her mother at one point plotted with the Mafia to have Margo killed herself. Margo had a pretty tough time believing that her mother would do that."

"Never having had a mother, I can't relate, but I'm sure you're right."

"But Margo was right," I corrected Haymeyer. "Her mother only intended to scare her, not to really have her shot."

"But that didn't make Margo feel a whole lot better, did it?" Shipman said.

Karlyn put her fingers to her temples.

"What is it?" Haymeyer asked.

She raised a hand to silence him, as if she were in deep thought. "I just remembered something I hadn't thought about in years. Not long after LaDonna got her paddling, little things began happening to my room and to my bed, even to my closet."

"Like what?" Shipman said. "Like what's been happening here lately?"

"Not exactly. One day my closet door was nailed shut. Once my bed was shortsheeted. Another time a tiny turtle was left in my shoe. I don't know if it relates or not. I hope not."

"Philip," Haymeyer said, standing, "let's bid Karlyn good night, thank Larry for his time, screw on the sliding door lock that will secure it against anyone, and head back to Glencoe."

Karlyn was shaky as she got our coats from the closet. Larry applied the lock, "just for precaution," and told her to call Earl if any messages turned up the next day.

"I don't really think any will," Shipman said. "Unless they appear on the patio. I believe we've secured the only logical point of entry."

"We'll see," Haymeyer said. "This intruder has been crafty. It may take more than being locked out to discourage him."

"Him?"

"Her?"

"It."

"Philip, I think you should go to Michigan first thing tomorrow."

"What'll I be looking for?"

"The whereabouts of the former LaDonna Finch. On the one hand, I hope you find she's migrated this way. On the other, for Karlyn's sake, I hope it's a dead end and we find it's just some neighborhood Peeping Tom we can scare off or put away."

I didn't know what to think. I believed in women's intuition, but it seemed Karlyn was just refusing to believe that her sweet little girl friend of so many years ago could have grown up into a bad woman. My only hope was that I could find someone at Creekside who would give me a solid lead.

There certainly were no other suspects. Although Karlyn had no close friends, she seemed to have no enemies either. Not one. Not even the man she had hit the last winter. When I finally reached him, telling him I represented her, he told me to assure her that he had been taken care of by her insurance company and was happy.

The reason it had taken so long for him to get back to me was that he had been in Bermuda for two weeks. "Unless he commuted to her patio every day," Haymeyer said, "he's not our man."

So who *was* our man? Initially I wanted to track him down because it was my first solo job. Then Shipman and Haymeyer had been so instrumental in leading me this far that I lost the thrill of its being my own. Now my whole motive was to help Karlyn out of her misery. I believed she was safe in her apartment with the intruder intent upon bothering her only when she was away.

When I called her the evening I arrived in Kalamazoo, however, I realized that time was not on our side.

"An envelope was in my mailbox when I got home," she said. "It had no stamp and no postmark. No letter either. Just a blank sheet of paper."

I called Haymeyer, who told me he would get out to Des Plaines to see if anyone had seen a stranger near the mailboxes that day, but that I should not hope for much. "At least that sliding door lock is forcing our target out into the open a little more," he said. "Let me know what you find up there."

I figured the bold approach would lead nowhere the next day, so I tried something different. "Does Mrs. Miller still work here?" I asked.

"No, but you may talk to Miss Bloom. She's headmistress now."

Before she would answer any questions, she wanted to know all about me, who I was, what I was doing in Michigan, and all the rest. I simply told her I was an artist who was in the area looking for a friend of a friend. I asked Miss Bloom if it ever happened that a girl who lived at Creekside came back to work there on the staff.

"Not very often, but there is a woman with us now who was here back in the sixties."

"Could I talk with her?"

"Certainly."

A few minutes later I rose to meet a slender, pleasant woman who introduced herself as Roberta Burns. "Did you know Karlyn May?" I asked her.

"I vaguely remember her," she said. "Are you a friend of hers?"

"Yes."

"Is she still a blonde?"

"Sure is. She has talked about a Mrs. Miller."

"Oh, yes."

"Whatever happened to her?"

"She retired. She lives only thirty miles or so from here."

"Would it be possible to get her address and phone number? I'd like to greet her for Karlyn."

"I think so."

When she returned with the information on a card, I thanked her and asked if she also remembered LaDonna Finch.

"Oh, who could forget!" she said.

"Unforgettable?" I said.

"That beautiful black hair," she said. "I never really knew her though. She was much younger than I. Caused a few problems around here before she left as I recall, though."

"Problems?"

"I wish I could remember. Seems to me she had been a cheery little thing and turned sullen. It happens to a lot of orphans, you know, at certain ages. Same was true with Karlyn when she became a teenager, as you probably know. I don't recall much of that story either, but I know she was transferred to the Chicago area for high school. Mrs. Miller will remember. She remembers them all."

SIXTEEN

I found Mrs. Miller in the tiny, former railroad round-house town of Constantine, Michigan. A robust, rawboned woman with silver hair, she was full of laughter and memories of "my girls."

She remembered Karlyn. "Of course. She and LaDonna Finch were extremely close for a while. They were such a pair, little blonde and black-haired sweeties, both with those unusual and beautiful names. They weren't the oldest or the smartest or even the most industrious girls in the home back then, but they were among the nicest and they were the favorites among the matrons."

"They were?"

"Yes, especially LaDonna. She had a lot going for her. She was not an unhappy girl until the time she was punished. It seemed to me that most of our workers were especially fond of her."

"But wasn't she *severely* punished?"

"Oh, yes, and I don't think she ever forgave Karlyn for that, though I can't imagine that it was entirely Karlyn's fault. LaDonna was punished by the one tough, little matron who resented the happiest girls, probably because she was not happy herself. We continually tried to weed out such women. We couldn't allow her to stay after that. We had hired her at a risk because she came with less than a perfect record at her previous job, which was at a girls' reformatory. I could never seem to get through to her that our girls were not at Creekside because of behavior problems."

"Has anyone ever told LaDonna what you just told me?"

"I doubt it. Of course, when you dismiss a woman like that, the girls never know why she's suddenly gone. They are not told what has happened."

"What ever happened to LaDonna?"

"She moved back with her mother to Grand Rapids. I was glad to see it. You always are when they are reunited with parents. And I was convinced her mother was a basically good, loving woman. I never did hear if she was able to get LaDonna back to normal."

"Back to normal?"

"Well, like I say, she was terribly hurt, and while we never had any direct evidence, we all knew that it was she who was pulling the dirty tricks on Karlyn, leaving things in her bed and what not. Oh, she was a motivated little girl. I never will know how she managed to nail that closet door shut." Mrs. Miller chuckled with the memory. I tried to.

"Karlyn still refuses to believe that LaDonna was capable of being mean."

"That's not surprising, Mr. Spence. But Karlyn should look at her own history. When she was told that her parents had been killed when she was three and that relatives who wished to remain anonymous had brought her to us, she demanded to know who they were and sulked for weeks when we would not tell her.

"The sweetest children change personalities. With Karlyn we had to recommend that she be transferred to an all-girls' home in Chicago when she became rebellious in her early teens. Of course, I got the word a few years ago that she had come around to be a mature young woman by the end of her high school years. You always love to hear that."

"And what did you hear of LaDonna?"

"You know, I never did hear much more about her and it always troubled me. She had more advantages than most of the other girls, especially more than Karlyn. Yet her pain was so deep, I don't suppose I could hope that she eventually became as well adjusted as many of the rebellious ones do. She did write to some of the girls at the home, though."

"Ever to Karlyn?"

"No, and that worried me. Once I even wrote to her mother, asking if she couldn't talk LaDonna into burying the hatchet with Karlyn. I never heard back from either mother or daughter, and as far as I know, Karlyn never heard from LaDonna again either."

I hoped that was true, but I feared it wasn't. I needed to know where LaDonna was now, but I knew Mrs. Miller couldn't be very specific. I probed carefully.

"So LaDonna's mother remarried and took her daughter home?"

"No, I believe she took LaDonna home when she realized that she wasn't going to find another husband who wanted a daughter. I'm convinced she left LaDonna at the orphanage to keep her out of her way while she searched for another husband, but she finally gave up. Whether she ever married after that, I wouldn't have any idea. I completely lost contact with that family once LaDonna's letters stopped coming. I only hope she found some happiness in this world. I couldn't tell you where she landed. Of course, I couldn't tell you if I knew, knowing of her problem with Karlyn."

I was brought up short. "Her problem with Karlyn?"

Now concentrating, I thought Mrs. Miller knew something I hadn't told her.

The old woman looked at me as if I were missing a strategic part. "Yes, the problem. Her silent treatment and the pranks—much too mild a word actually—before LaDonna moved home."

"Of course."

Mrs. Miller asked me to greet Karlyn for her and thanked me for the conversation. "I always enjoy reminiscing about my girls," she said, "though I have lost contact with so many of them. Many still write me, you know. Tell Karlyn she should do that."

"I will," I promised, but right then I was anxious to get to Grand Rapids. I had to find that girl.

As soon as I got inside the Grand Rapids city limits, I stopped in a phone booth and wrestled the phone book around so I could look up the Finches. I didn't know what the odds were that LaDonna had not married or if there was a Finch anywhere who would know what became of her or her mother, and the phone book didn't help much either. The first half of it had been torn apart. As long as I was there I checked in with Earl. It was good that I did.

"Time is a problem, Philip," he said. "Karlyn received another message last night. It was a letter, not hand delivered this time but mailed from Park Ridge. It said, 'How would you like to have *your* seat paddled until it bleeds?'"

"And I had begun wondering what I was doing in Michigan while Karlyn was in trouble in Illinois."

"Still wondering?"

"Hardly."

"Don't let me keep you from finding a phone book," Earl said.

"I want to call Karlyn and Margo real quick," I said. "And then I'll be back on the trail."

"Good luck."

I then telephoned Karlyn at her office.

"I'm not doing too well," she admitted. "But Earl said there was no way he'd leave me alone once he decides that something is about to happen."

"Of course we wouldn't leave you alone, Karlyn. In fact I hope to be back in time to help."

"I hope you are too," she said.

"I'll be praying for you, Karlyn, and I know Margo will be too."

"I appreciate that, Philip."

I called Margo. She was having no luck finding a job in Pontiac. "If I don't find something soon," she said, "I don't know if I can stay here. I'm not going to take just any old job. There are waitress jobs galore, but I've been that route before."

"If that means you might come back to Chicago and find work that would pay you enough so you could make weekly trips to Pontiac, I couldn't be happier," I said.

"That would be quite a job, Philip. If you find one like that for me, let me know."

When I told her what was happening in my search, she scolded me for letting her ramble about "my petty problems. You'd better find yourself a phone book and get to work."

I finally found a phone book intact, but there were no LaDonna Finches. Remembering Margo's telling me that single women often have themselves listed under an initial only so no one can tell that it's a woman, I checked under the Ls for LaDonna and the Ds for just Donna. There were several D. Finches along with the Finch Day Care Center, Finch Dog Hotel, and Finch Dress Boutique, but I decided to start with the half-dozen L. Finches and hope for the best.

After getting four embarrassing responses to my asking for LaDonna—and wondering if I wouldn't have done better to study mechanical drawing by mail than to be in "our kind of work" as Haymeyer always called it—my break came.

"LaDonna won't be back for three more days," a man's voice said.

"Who am I talking to, please?" I said.

"You're talking to Frank. I'm just looking after the place while LaDonna's away. It's the first time nobody's been in this house for years."

"Frank, could I talk to you for a little while? I have just a few questions for you. I'm a friend of an old friend of LaDonna's."

"I haven't talked to anyone for so long, I might enjoy that."

Following his directions, I pulled into a long driveway that led to a modest, two-story frame house set far back from the road. Frank was in the yard clipping hedges.

"You said it's been a long time since nobody's been in the house," I began. "What did you mean by that?"

"Ever since old man Finch died years and years ago, Mrs. Finch's been livin' here. Her daughter LaDonna's been with her now nearly twenty more, takin' care of her mama since she took sick here a few years ago. All that in spite of LaDonna's workin' downtown. Now that she's gone, who knows what LaDonna'll do? She never did marry, ya know."

"You say her mother's gone now?"

"Yep. Died 'bout four, five weeks ago. Right after the funeral LaDonna hired me to house-sit and tend the yard. Told me she'd be back in exactly five weeks."

"And that's three days from now?"

"Yessir."

"Frank, where did she go?"

"Believe she went to Indiana, maybe Illinois."

"She didn't tell you where she could be reached?"

"Nope, just had me get her a map that showed Interstate 94 West. That'll take you just about anywhere you want to go, startin' here and goin' through Indiana and Illinois."

I thanked Frank and headed back to my car. "Who should I say come callin'?" he asked.

I stopped. "For ten bucks would you not say anyone called?"

"Sure thing. Thanks."

I figured I'd be seeing LaDonna before he did anyway.

SEVENTEEN

I had just reentered Illinois when I stopped to call Earl and breathlessly told him everything I had discovered.

"Did you happen to find out what line of work LaDonna's in that allows her to take off that amount of time?"

"No, why?"

"Well, it would be good to know where she works so we could see if she has psychological problems now, if she's hard to work with or moody or whatever."

"Do you think we have time, Earl?"

"Probably not. I've sensed all along that the harassment has been building to something more ominous. That note about the paddling had to be a promise of action."

"What are we going to do?"

"I'll think about it. You get back here."

Shipman was in Haymeyer's office when I arrived. "I want help on this thing," Haymeyer explained.

"Great," I said. "It's getting good, Larry."

Haymeyer said he would like to be with Karlyn when she got home from work, so we called her and then drove to Des Plaines to follow her home from her office. In her mail was a letter postmarked Park Ridge again. She opened it as we all stood in the hall. It read: "When I really want in, I can get in."

When Karlyn opened the door to her apartment, a cold gust of wind hit us. The glass on one of the two patio doors had been cut. It lay in huge pieces, obviously done with a glass cutter and suction cup that allowed the intruder to break it without a lot of noise and just lay the pieces down without shattering them. "Stay right here," Haymeyer said.

He and Shipman entered the apartment, Earl's gun drawn. I followed a few steps behind. No one was there and nothing seemed to have been touched, except that the wind had blown open the pages of the magazine on the coffee table in the living room.

"Ship, get on the phone and get someone in here to board up that door."

"Why wouldn't anything have been taken or changed?" Karlyn asked, shaken.

"It was just a message," Haymeyer said. "By now she knows we could stake out the bushes. Maybe she subconsciously wants to get caught."

"I hope you'll oblige her," Karlyn said.

"Don't worry," Earl said. "I think we've got her right where we want her. The problem now is, we can't let you stay here alone anymore. She could make her move anytime. What I want to do is cut down her options. If she really has to be back to Michigan in a few days—and if we knew what her job was we would know for sure—let's give her only one chance at getting you before then. For the next two nights I want you to stay in a hotel in Glencoe. You'll come back here every day after work to get your mail, and then you'll leave right away."

"Whatever you say, Earl. But then what?"

"The next day you can return with your clothes and everything, making it very obvious that you're back home to stay. My hope is that she'll think you feel confident to move back in and that'll give her just that night to do whatever she's going to do."

"And I'm the live bait?"

"You won't be alone. We'll come to your apartment during the day from various directions and even different floors. We'll stay out of sight of the windows, and when you come home, talk to us only in whispers and don't look at us. We want it to appear to anyone watching that you are alone as usual. Then when you go to bed, you will have one of us in the other room. Fair enough?"

"And when someone starts to break in?"

"We wait until she's committed herself, is fully inside, and obviously looking to do you bodily harm."

"How will you know that? When she's in my room with a knife at my throat?"

"We won't let her get that far."

"I don't know about this."

"It's the only way, Karlyn, unless you'd like us to use a stand-in for you."

"How about a dummy like you did for Margo in Atlanta?" I asked.

"This isn't set up for that, Philip," Earl said. "We don't know where this girl might be watching from or when. We have to assume she knows Karlyn's comings and goings. She's been right every day for weeks."

"But her time's running out," Shipman said. "Here's hoping your idea works, Earl. It would be nice to be able to catch her in the act so you can put her away for a while."

"Or get her some help," Karlyn said.

"You sound just like Margo," I said. "She always felt more for her pursuer than any of the rest of us. Personally I think what this girl has done to you already is nearly unforgivable."

"She probably feels the same about what she thinks I did to her years ago, but knowing God allows me to be able to somehow feel pity even for one who would torment me. Don't you pity her?"

Karlyn searched each of our eyes for the sympathy she hoped to find for LaDonna. Sad to say, she didn't find much. "Philip," she said, "you of all people should feel something for her."

I nodded lamely. Why was it that women like Margo and Karlyn seemed to have more depth of Christian character than I did? It bothered me for the next two days while Karlyn commuted from Glencoe to Des Plaines each day and often badgered me about having such feelings of animosity toward LaDonna.

She received no letter on either day, but when she stopped in at her apartment for a moment the second day after work, the telephone was ringing. "Don't cross me up now," a woman's voice said, and the line went dead. Karlyn ran down to her car and sped to Glencoe.

"I didn't know you were going to your apartment," Earl said. "It wasn't smart. You should have told us. It's obvious she knows when you're there and when you're not."

The next afternoon, the day before LaDonna was expected back in Michigan, Karlyn returned to her own apartment after work. "We're here," Haymeyer said from next to me in the closet when she came in.

"Hello," she whispered.

"And I'm in the corner of the kitchen," Larry said. "Don't be alarmed when you see me."

"I won't."

It was weird to be stationed in her apartment, out of sight of the windows and the door. "What should I do now?" Karlyn asked quietly without looking at anyone.

"Whatever you normally do," Haymeyer said, reclining

next to me on the floor of the closet with a blanket and a pillow, reading a magazine.

During the course of the evening while Karlyn puttered around the apartment trying to look normal, she called Margo in Pontiac. She passed along Margo's love and reported that she was close to landing a job much like Karlyn's at a local printing plant. "She'll know tomorrow. And she can't see her mother for another several days. Mrs. Franklin has the flu or something."

"Oh, great," I said.

By about eleven o'clock, Earl and I were stiff and sore, Shipman was not where he could move much either. Our whispering had quit and Karlyn was getting ready for bed. "I'm getting a little nervous," she said.

"So are we," Earl said. "If you're not nervous now, you're not human."

"I must not be human," Shipman said quietly. "I'm excited."

"You're right," Earl said. "You've never been human. You're an animal."

"I usually shut the closet before I go to bed," Karlyn said.

"Come and shut it then," Earl replied.

"You're going to stay in there with the door shut?"

"Just shut it and go to bed. There are slats for air and we can hear. If she sees the closet door open, knowing how persnickety you are, she'll smell a rat."

"I won't be able to sleep," Karlyn said.

"No kidding," Larry said. "But unless you hear us leave, you can rest assured we'll be here. And we won't be sleeping either."

"Thanks, you guys," she said, sounding more like a little girl than I had ever heard her. "And be careful, OK?"

"To bed," Haymeyer said.

About an hour later Karlyn's phone rang. She answered

it on the extension in her room. The caller immediately hung up. She rose without turning on the light. "What do you suppose that was all about, Earl?" she whispered from the doorway.

"Probably just making sure you're here," he said. "Be patient and try to stay calm. We could have company soon."

Just before one o'clock Earl and I heard footsteps in the hall that stopped just outside the door. "I didn't figure her for the front door tonight," Haymeyer whispered. From the kitchen came the faint sounds of Shipman jockeying for a better position to see and hear.

A note was slipped under the door and the footsteps retreated. I started to get up to get the note, but Haymeyer put a hand on my shoulder. "Let's give it a few minutes," he said.

"What's happening?" Karlyn asked. Shipman shushed her. We waited several minutes in silence. No one moved. Then we heard the patio railing squeak, so lightly that we wouldn't have heard it if we hadn't half expected it.

Haymeyer tried to get into position to see the patio through the slats in the closet door. "No good," he whispered. "But let's not move unless she comes in." We heard feet lightly touch the concrete.

"I can see her on the patio," Shipman whispered. "Small, wiry, lithe. It's her all right. She's leaning against the boarded-up side."

Something touched the glass and made scratching sounds. "What in the world is she doing?" I asked, barely audibly.

"She's probably cutting glass again." He was right. She tapped lightly until a piece came loose, held in a rubber suction cup. She now had a hole big enough to allow her to reach in and unscrew the sliding door lock Shipman had installed.

Haymeyer drew his gun and rolled up onto the balls of his feet, knees bent. "Keep me posted, Ship," he breathed. "I'm ready to move. Sit tight, Philip."

Gladly, I thought.

We heard nothing. Then Shipman was moving toward the closet in direct view of the window. "What are you doing?" Haymeyer scolded.

"Earl, she's gone," he said. "She cut that glass and left it hanging on the suction cup, and then she just turned and jumped over the railing again. She's gone."

Haymeyer swore. "Leave the lights off. She may be back. This time we'll wait for her in the kitchen, all of us. If she comes in, I'll take her right then. Let's see that note."

I brought it to him, and he held it up to a thin shaft of light coming through the window. "It's just a matter of time," it read.

"She didn't expect Karlyn to get this until morning," Haymeyer said. "Is it possible that she's smarter than to try anything inside the apartment?"

"She's been pretty crafty so far," Shipman said. "Maybe this whole apartment assault has been a ruse."

"When is this going to end?" Karlyn asked. "You can't hold my hand the rest of my life."

"I hope it ends when we force it to," Earl said. "Not when she does. Meanwhile, let's get some sleep."

EIGHTEEN

Shipman taped the hole in the window and traded off standing watch with Haymeyer and me. Karlyn hardly slept.

While she got ready for work, I called Margo. "I want you to come up here between now and the time you have to start your job," I said. "I can't take it anymore."

"That's good to hear," she said. "I don't have any money, but I'll scrape some up somewhere. I'm bored to death here with nothing to do, and there's a lot I want to talk about. Living this far apart just isn't going to make it."

"My sentiments exactly. When will you be leaving for Glencoe?"

"Within the hour, love."

"If you get there before I do, just wait for me at Earl's office. I don't know when we'll be free today. Earl thinks it's going to break soon. I'll see you then."

As we waited I felt again for Margo and all that she had been through. It was unfair that so much of her life had been eaten up by the problems of her mother. And now those apron strings had reached right out of the prison walls and ensnared her again.

Tonight when I saw her again, I would take Margo to the same place we had been to a few days before she left. I would tell her all that I had been thinking about, and I would try to be as articulate as she had been the last time.

If I could somehow express to her all that she meant to me and how much I loved her and needed her, perhaps we could work out something more equitable than living more than a hundred miles apart. Especially if we were married. That is, if she would say yes.

By tonight I would know. She wouldn't be expecting the question, but like Earl had said so many times, "You're not kids anymore." I wanted to get this settled before she accepted any job offer in Pontiac. I couldn't wait to see her.

Earl's voice brought me back to the situation at hand. "We have to decide how we're going to keep an eye on Karlyn today. We shouldn't let her out of our sight. Larry, why don't you start by bringing my car around."

Karlyn was pale and shaky. "I'm going to be good for nothing at work today." Dressed and ready to go, she sat at the kitchen table as if waiting for the coast to clear. "Are you going to follow me, or what?"

"At least," Haymeyer said. "I'm not sure what to do with you at work and at lunch and all."

Shipman tapped at the door. I let him in and he said, "Earl, let me see you for a minute." They went into Karlyn's bedroom and shut the door. Karlyn looked at me. I shrugged.

As the door opened again Earl was saying, "Yeah, ask her."

"Do you ever leave your car unlocked or a window open just a fraction?"

"Never."

"Not even yesterday afternoon when you were thinking about finding us in your apartment when you arrived?"

"No way."

"Well," Shipman said with a sigh, "the window on the passenger's side is down about a quarter of an inch and the windows are slightly fogged. Do you have that problem as a rule?"

"Only in the dead of winter. Never in the spring."

"Someone's in the car?" I said.

"Excellent, Philip," Shipman said, rolling his eyes.

Haymeyer looked at both of us as if to say, Shut up and let me think. "Feel brave this morning, Karlyn?" he said.

"How brave?"

"Brave enough to walk to your car as if everything is normal?"

"And where will you be?"

"We'll casually converge on your car, all at about the same time you get to it. Rather than opening the door, I want you to just drop to your knees by the left rear tire. Philip will be there at the same time. Just stay there until it's over."

"How do I get there?" I asked.

"Hold on. I'll get to you."

"And what if she just shoots me as I come near the car?" Karlyn asked.

"She wouldn't be that stupid. Try to get away in the car of the person you've just shot?"

"Anyway," Larry said, "there's no one in the front seat. I walked right by the car. She's in no position to hot-wire the car and take off."

"I'm putting my life in your hands," Karlyn said.

"It's totally up to you, kid," Haymeyer said. "We could just charge out there and storm the car, but I'd feel a whole lot better about it if her attention was on you rather than us when we make our move."

"That's just what I don't want—her attention on me."

"It's been on you for weeks," Haymeyer said. "That's why you won't actually get into the car. If you're kneeling where I told you, she would have to climb over the front seat and out the door to get to you. By that time I've got her."

Karlyn sat thinking, fists clenched. "I'll do it," she said. "I'm tired of this and I want it over." She stood.

Haymeyer said, "Are you ready?"

"Sure, boss," I said. "Where do you want me?"

"Just take the elevator up three floors, exit right and walk down the stairs to the exit at the end of the building. We'll watch from the window in the stairwell at this end. When you get outside, we'll send Karlyn from this exit. Try to time it so you reach the car from behind when she gets there from this end. Our friend in the car should never see you, Philip. When you both are about twenty steps from the car, Ship and I will get in my car and start a slow U-turn. We will appear to be pulling away, but as we get near Karlyn's car, Larry will pull in front of it and stop.

"Everybody got it?"

We all nodded.

"Ready?"

We nodded again and I moved out to the elevator. I stepped on and pushed the button for the fifth floor to the glare of the other passengers who knew before I did that the car was going down. I had to step out and let them all off at the first floor, then reboard and ride up to five.

I hurried down the hall on the fifth floor and took the stairs down two at a time. Going down isn't supposed to be as exhausting as going up, but I realized when I hit the ground floor that I had held my breath most of the way. Now I was huffing and puffing as I burst out the door.

"Help me calm down, Lord," I prayed. "Slow me down, don't let me blow it." I tried to shorten my stride despite my crashing chest and shortness of breath, but my knees were rubbery. I must have looked like a toy, bouncing along the parking lot.

Karlyn came out of her exit holding her purse and a small attaché case to her chest with both arms. She, too, was trying to look casual and not doing a good job of it.

Her car keys were lodged between her fingers. I slowed a bit so we would be about equidistant from her car. I tingled from the backs of my knees all the way up to my neck. She walked faster. I sped up. We were probably thirty steps from her car when Shipman and Haymeyer came out and got into Earl's car without even glancing our way.

I knew Ship was watching us in the rearview mirror. When we drew closer, Shipman shifted into drive and slowly pulled ahead. He looked over his shoulder and began a wide, slow U-turn. I glanced at Karlyn's car. I saw the slight fogging of the windows, but nothing else.

As Karlyn heard Shipman and Haymeyer coming she hesitated and almost turned to look. I held my breath. She kept moving. Just as she pretended to reach toward the door with her key, I noticed movement in the car and dropped to my knees by the rear tire.

I grabbed the arm of Karlyn's coat and she tumbled on top of me, burying her face in my shoulder as the driver's side door opened.

Shipman screeched to a stop in front of the car as Haymeyer skittered out and around to our side, sliding neatly to one knee with both hands on his gun. "Freeze!" he screamed. "Hold it right there!"

Karlyn pressed closer to me and over her shoulder I saw a woman's hand push the car door all the way open. She was prone across the back of the front seat and had been about to come out headfirst when Haymeyer confronted her. Now Shipman joined Earl and approached the car. All I could see was the woman's outstretched arms. In her right hand was an old wood paddle.

"This gal is more than two years older than you are, Karlyn," Haymeyer announced as he and Shipman pulled the hysterical woman into view, her feet trailing across the seat.

"I almost had you, you little brat!" she managed through her sobs.

Karlyn's head shot around.

"You're in trouble, young lady!" the woman shrieked as Earl and Larry wrestled her into Haymeyer's car. "You got me fired!"

"Miss Kepkey!" Karlyn gasped. "It's Miss Kepkey!"

"One of the things that really intrigues me," an exhausted Karlyn said a few hours later in Earl's office, "is where LaDonna was all this time."

"Me too," Haymeyer said, looking my way.

"Hey, did I do something wrong?" I asked. "What would you have done with the same information?"

"Probably the same, Philip. Don't feel bad. But I'm betting that a little *more* information would have changed the picture some. Call the Finch home and see if she's arrived."

A woman answered.

"Miss Finch?" I said.

"Who's calling, please?"

"My name is Philip Spence. I'm a friend of Karlyn May."

"Pardon me?"

"Karlyn May."

"That's what I thought you said. Let me sit down. Who did you say *you* were?"

"Philip Spence."

"And you know Karlyn?"

"Yes, ma'am."

"Do you know that I've been looking for Karlyn for years? She was my best friend when I was a kid, but something happened and we lost contact. How did you get my number? How did you know I knew Karlyn? I—"

"Do you want to talk to Karlyn yourself?"

"Why, yes!"

"Let me ask you something first, if I may. Where have you been the last five weeks?"

"Vacationing in Wisconsin. You see, my mother died recently and I just had to get away. I needed a long break from home and work, and my assistants are able to handle my day-care center."

"Just a minute please, LaDonna. Karlyn, it's for you."

While she was on the phone, Margo arrived.

"Got any plans for lunch?" I said.

"Hardly. Is that an invitation?"

"Unlike any you've ever had," I said. "Keep your coat on."

ABOUT THE AUTHOR

Jerry Jenkins is a widely published author of biographies and fiction. He has written the biographies of Orel Hershiser (on the New York Times Bestseller list for nine weeks), Meadowlark Lemon, Hank Aaron, Walter Payton, B.J. Thomas, Dick Motta, Luis Palau, and Deanna McClary.

Many of Jenkins' ninety books have topped the religious bestseller lists.

His writing has been published in *Reader's Digest, The Saturday Evening Post,* and virtually every major Christian magazine.

Jenkins is currently writer-in-residence at Moody Bible Institute. Born in Kalamazoo, Michigan, Jenkins lives in the country, near Zion, Illinois, with his wife, Dianna, and their three sons, Dallas, Chad, and Michael.